Sydney On Fire

Sydney on FIRE

a novel

B. B. Cary

GAB DATE PRODUCTIONS, LLC
DELAWARE • NEW YORK

Sydney on Fire

Copyright © 2017 by B. B. Cary

All rights reserved. Published by Gab Date Productions, LLC.
No part of this book may be used, reproduced, scanned, or distributed in any printed or electronic form without written permission except in the case of brief quotations embodied in critical articles and reviews. For information regarding permission, contact Gab Date Productions, LLC at gaddate@verizon.net.

This is a work of fiction. Names, characters, places, and incidents are either the product of the author's imagination or are used fictitiously, and any resemblance to actual persons, living or dead, business establishments, events, or locales is entirely coincidental. The publisher does not have any control over and does not assume any responsibility for third-party websites or their content.

Interior Book Design and Formatting by Rachel Reiss
Book Cover Design by Ursa Minor Design
Editorial Guidance by Jami Bernard/Barncat Publishing Inc.

trade paperback ISBN 978-0-9988293-0-2
LCCN 2017943775
ebook ISBN 978-0-9988293-1-9

For Sydney's Squad

"It is not only what we do, but also what we do not do, for which we are accountable."
—MOLIÈRE

One

THERE SHE STOOD—a scrap in the middle of a circle of vultures. With half-closed eyes and her mouth ajar, she weaved and tilted, then stopped. Folded over at the waist, she hung her head low, a few inches from the steamy pavement. She froze. Seconds later, she jerked back up. Forward and back, forward and nearly over, and halfway up again. Long, silky black hair shrouded her sculpted cheekbones and nearly camouflaged her coal rimmed Asian eyes.

At two A.M., Tompkins Square Park in New York City's East Village was dark with a blue-black hue. Broken street lamps cast dim yellow spheres on the chopped-up pavement. It was tropical hot on this August night. The air smelled of vomit and rancid bodega takeout.

The circle of four men closed in. The woman clutched her bag fiercely to her chest, the leather strap wound tightly around her wrist. A quick hand with filthy broken nails reached out to snatch it. Shuffling back, she hugged it closer. Another man advanced. She zigzagged. *Smack!* Her head snapped to the side as his open hand slapped her cheek. She was down. MAC lipsticks, a pack of Marlboros, and a gold lighter flew out of her Louis Vuitton.

"Get the bag and whatever else," a male voice instructed. "Stupid yellow bitch. Dumb-ass junkie."

A dull thud and the loudmouth fell. A rapid, back-fist whack and another man dropped. The two still upright flinched and swiveled. One shouted, "What the...?" The men surrounded the black-clad, leather-gloved figure. One took it in the face; the other got it in the knees. Both fell; one groaned. A front snap kick delivered to the groaner stopped that noise.

The park was quiet again. Walking over to the skeletal, curled-up form, the stranger bent down, checked the woman's pulse, then draped the body over her shoulders like a wounded calf.

The loudest of the pack moaned, "You dead, bitch." A back kick to his chin restored the silence as they exited.

Hollowed-eyed, zombielike inhabitants bordering the park mumbled as the rescuer hauled the unconscious woman north, up Avenue B. Night crawlers leaning against grimy bar windows smoked cigarettes and stared.

"Maybe you can carry me around too, sweet thang!" said a shirtless man holding a sweaty beer can. On Twenty-First and Second, she turned left; then right before the police station, she located the matching LV keychain in the woman's handbag and entered a white brick apartment building.

Inside Apartment J on the eighth floor, she moved through the shadowy foyer and set the body down on the worn linoleum tiling. Ripping off leather gloves, exposing purple surgical ones, she stripped the woman's soiled clothes and rolled them into a ball with her foot. Kicking off her sneakers, she picked up the naked body and continued through the foyer and around the bend. A quick flick of her elbow switched on the light as they entered a bright red bedroom.

She pulled back the gold-and-blue Chinese embroidered bedspread and laid the body down, then flung the handbag's shoulder strap around the doorknob. From the linen closet, she grabbed a washcloth and cleaned caked-up drool from the woman's slack mouth. Rolling the body onto its belly, she tucked her in. Another pulse check—steady.

In the 1960s-era kitchen, she wrapped a plastic bag around her hand and picked up the bundle of clothing, shoved it into another bag, tied it, and tossed it onto a half-sized washing machine. She poured bleach onto the foyer floor and wiped it dry with a swath of paper towels under her feet. Tossing her gloves into a tarnished garbage can, she washed her hands for a full minute. Back in her sneakers, she approached the front door.

"Is everything okay, Sydney?" an older, groggy voice called out.

"Yes."

"Did you find your sister?"

"Yes, Ma."

Two

On her own condo lobby, six blocks south, Sydney removed her baseball cap, and ice-cold air caressed her closely shaved head. On coral Italian marble floors, Sydney passed gold-flecked walls and sleek leather couches as she nodded to Mike, the sleepy concierge.

"Night."

"Morning," he replied with a yawn and grin.

Sydney kicked her grimy "outside" sneakers onto a wad of old newspaper that sat by her apartment door. The interior walls were matte white. A card table, two fold-up chairs, and a leather lounger were in the living room. A wall unit filled with books and a Duxiana bed with an assortment of barbells peeking out from underneath sat in the bedroom. Above the bed hung a poster-sized painting of a frog by a young, enthusiastic artist.

In the stark white bathroom, inches from the mirror, she started her "after Lily" routine. She checked her symmetrically shaped head for abrasions. Clean. Stepping into a steamy hot shower, she scrubbed the thin layer of petroleum from her café-au-lait-complexioned face and neck. Sydney always greased before searching for her sister; it prevented cuts from an occasional surprise punch. *It's starting again. But she's been clean for a year. At least I think she has.* It was the longest good stretch she'd had since she'd started mainlining at fifteen. She was the good girl, the obedient daughter. The one voted "Most Likely to Succeed." Sydney was the one in the principal's office every day. Even drugged, Lily was brilliant. She was at the top of her mortuary school class. *What a waste.*

Minutes later, Sydney hung upside down from the metal chin-up bar in her bedroom's doorway. She read *Naked Statistics* hanging by both legs, then just her right, then left. When the chapter was finished, she flipped over and off.

Three

SYDNEY STRAPPED ON inline skates. It was another scorcher. Turning her acid-green cap backward, she tore across Fifteenth Street in slate-colored mirrored sunglasses, leggings, and a sleeveless top.

It was the same route every day. Park Avenue South, to Madison, to Fifty-Ninth Street past the Plaza Hotel, and a quick right into the shadowy wilderness of Central Park. An ethereal, Zen-like serenity welcomed her as a gentle breeze kissed her nose. With her torso bent, her core taut, arms swinging rhythmically, and her head in perfect alignment, she was in the sweet spot. Birdcalls, insect buzzes, and rustling leaves transported her back to her childhood days, when she and Johnny endlessly roamed the woods surrounding her family's country cabin in upstate New York.

Sydney's only childhood friend, Johnny, had knocked on her front door at dawn every day during the summer, and on weekend mornings throughout rest of the year. She'd wait for him with a backpack stuffed with peanut butter and jelly sandwiches and purple grape juice. They'd play in the forest until dusk, speaking sparingly, crafting bows and arrows, fishing, and climbing rocks. When the sun went down, they'd return to their respective homes across the street from each other.

Sydney inhaled deeply.

No vehicles were allowed in this part of the park. She raced with stronger and longer strides. *It was much easier when Lily was sixteen; the rich guys at those parties didn't fight, couldn't fight. Now it's street thugs. I'm so tired of being the muscle, but that's what I was raised to be.* Flying out of the park, she continued east on Seventy-Second Street. Hoots, honks, and catcalls chased her, but since age eleven, she'd tuned them out.

A door burst open from a parked SUV into the bike lane, and she swerved. A quick spin left her close to the offending vehicle. Her outstretched fist pounded the roof as the driver leaned in to grab something.

Zen was over as rush hour forced its way in.

Stopped at a coffee stand on the corner of First Avenue, she glanced across the street.

"Morning. Coffee, OJ, a powdered donut, a bottle of water in one bag—times two, please."

Skating across, she bent over and handed a bag to a man lying on the soot-filled grate.

"Morning, Mr. Johnson."

"Hot one today, baby. How you doin', pretty lady?"

Sirens screamed, trucks belched dropping off food to neighborhood stores, and taxis jockeyed for pickups. Sydney skated among a continuous stream of cars pulling in and out of side streets. She turned right onto Eighty-Second Street, half a block off the East River.

"What's up?" a buff man in a sky-blue jumpsuit called out.

"Morning, Leroy."

Screeching to an abrupt halt as a car pulled away from the curb in front of her workplace, she checked her watch. *Twenty minutes behind schedule. No time to sit on the curb and read.*

A distinguished gentleman in a starched lab coat, well-cut slacks, and brown suede shoes approached.

"Good morning, Sydney."

"Morning," she said without looking up. Removing her cap, she grabbed the water bottle and poured it over her head and into her mouth. Two white deli napkins blotted the wetness from her scalp and face as the staff stood around chitchatting. She leaned against the wall, removed her skates, and, with socks and sandals in place, walked toward the side entrance of Manhattan Hospital—the oldest, most prestigious hospital in New York City.

A parked ambulance swirled its lights, and a nurse hurried by.

"Morning, Dr. Chang."

four

PINK MARBLED FLOORING, thirty-foot ceilings, and sandstone walls made the main entrance look like a grand ballroom. Scattered vases filled with fresh flowers and museum-quality old-world paintings created a five-star-hotel feel. She thought about grabbing an espresso at the café, off to the left, but it was already jammed.

The phone was ringing as she dropped her skates in her eight-by-seven-foot, windowless office. Without looking, she grabbed it.

"Did you like your surprise?" asked Hasina, also an anesthesiologist, ten years her senior. Sydney hung the skates over her chair.

"Surprise?" Sydney removed her soaked socks.

"Yes. Are you really that cold-blooded?" Hasina asked with her singsong lilt.

"Yes. But what surprise?" She reached for clean scrubs from a shelf.

"Robbie. Isn't my baby in your office?"

"No." Sydney stood still.

"Well, he should be," Hasina said.

five

"E'S NOT THERE? That guy is going to get it. I told him not to wander," Hasina said.

"Backtrack. Why *would* he be here at seven A.M.?"

"Martyn took the kids hiking for four days. I kept Robbie home because of day camp, plus they didn't want him complaining all the way up the mountain and all the way down. You know the way he can get."

Sydney was silent.

"So that little prankster is not there. I'll kill him."

"Not here. He walked up here from your office, alone?" Sydney asked with narrowed eyes.

"Yes."

"How long ago? I just got here."

"Uh, about fifteen minutes. You're late today. What's up?"

"Not late. Just behind."

"Oh, what happened?"

"Nothing. And why are you here? It's Tuesday. I thought you were off today."

"I was. But remember when I promised Marlene, the nurse from peds, that I'd do her epidural when the time came? Well, the time came at five this morning. Story of my life. So

I grabbed Robbie, figured I'd take him to work, then Mickey D's, then camp. Anyway, Robbie wanted to surprise you. Probably ran off to get a Snickers or something. Or maybe he's hiding in an OR. I told him he was only to go to your office, no cafeteria, no running around, no hiding in the ORs. And now, well... Oh, and to make matters worse, don't expect any coffee today. The coffee machine is out once again!"

"Stop talking, Hasina. I'm hanging up. Go look for him. Maybe he's lost."

"Don't be ridiculous! He's been roaming this hospital since he could crawl. Believe me, he knows his way around better than most of the doctors; definitely better than me."

Sydney looked at Robbie's photos on her wall and smiled. He was her best buddy—her only buddy. The day she met him was a cold Sunday, around Christmas. Hasina had asked her to join them for dinner. The three older boys were playing a video game, and five-year-old Robbie was sulking in his room. No one wanted to play with him. Sydney plopped onto his floor, and together they built an airplane from LEGOs. From that day on, they coined themselves "Team Trouble," which made his siblings jealous. That made Robbie happy. Sydney, too.

She was excited to see Robbie. She usually just saw him on Sundays, when they Rollerbladed and rock climbed in Central Park. The thought of seeing his face for even a few minutes during the week brightened her entire day.

She knew exactly what Hasina was doing now. First, she'd adjust her too-tight, extra-large blue scrubs. Then she'd bend over her desk and take another bite of her second powdered donut of the morning. She'd wash it down with dark, sweet coffee brought from home in a thermos, brush the white powdered sugar off of her bosom, and reapply bright red lipstick to her full lips. Finally, she'd push her chair out from underneath the desk.

Sydney grabbed the fresh scrubs and walked to the bathroom. She wiped her body down with a damp towel and dried off with another. Reentering her office, she checked her voice mail. A deep, gravelly, nicotine-battered voice blurted out. Lily, hysterical, something about stabbing her cat by mistake while trimming his fur, and he was bleeding. The message was two days old. She heard it when it came through but never deleted it. Sydney grimaced, pressed reset, and slid into her neon green work sneakers.

Sydney rode the elevator down to the second floor. Walking the equivalent of two city blocks, she turned left, whizzing through massive white doors to Hasina's office. "Where's the kid?" she asked as she entered. Hasina was looking into a small hand mirror, combing her thick, wavy black hair. She favored her aristocratic Egyptian father's looks way more than her blond, blue-eyed Australian mother's. Robbie was her polar opposite, looks-wise. A combination of his Austrian father and his Australian grandmother, he was light-skinned and blond with crystal blue eyes. His brothers had light skin with dark eyes and black hair.

"I have no idea. Looks like he took some change from the bowl on my desk. I'll start with the cafeteria. Oh, by the way, sorry, your first case is Margaret Merriweather, a VIP." Sydney scowled. "Who's the surgeon?"

"Evans."

"Ugh."

"I know. I know. Why do they need you when the patient picked a mediocre surgeon? But, Sydney, they don't want any mishaps. She's a big donor. I tried to get you out of it, but they insisted on you. Try to be nice to her, but civil will do. And don't forget to keep your mask up so they don't see you making rat lip." Hasina popped a mini chocolate chip cookie into her mouth.

"Put down the cookies and find your son, Hasina."

"I'm going, I'm going. Oh, you wouldn't believe the e-mail I just got."

"Hasina, go."

"No, let me just tell you this. A patient wrote a complaint saying he never met an anesthesiologist named Hasina Wagner. He said a lovely little fat man came to talk to him the night before and then did his anesthetic. Well, I looked at his chart, and I did both. So I wrote him back: 'I am that lovely little fat man; please pay my bill.' Can you believe that?"

Sydney coughed over a guffaw. "Stop by OR Six when you get him. I'll come out and say hi."

"Will do. But can you believe the nerve of that patient?"

"It happens, Hasina. Remember when I was described as Mediterranean and elegant?"

"Yes, but at least that was a compliment."

THE HALLWAYS BUZZED with morning activity. Perioperative patient assistants, PPAs, formerly called orderlies, pushed big steel units full of OR equipment. Nurses and nursing assistants flew in and out of locker rooms, then searched for the proper supplies to set up their ORs. Some were busy finalizing paperwork and taking vital signs. When finished, they escorted their patients into designated operating rooms. Anesthesia personnel input codes, pulled out drawers, and grabbed fistfuls of drugs. They unlocked large tray units and set up their medicines and instruments.

Sydney was ready to start when the nurse entered with the patient. She rolled a chair over to the OR table as Mrs. Merriweather sat down.

"Hello. I'm Dr. Chang from anesthesia. Your consent form says you are having a hysteroscopy and a D and C. Is that correct?"

"Yes."

Sydney nodded in her blue surgical cap and mask as she reviewed her chart. "Do you have any allergies, Mrs. Merriweather?"

"No."

"Have you had anesthesia before?"

"Yes."

"Any problems?"

"Well, I became nauseated."

"I'll do my best to make sure that doesn't happen again. Any health problems or medications?"

"No."

"I'm going to start an intravenous line. Then I'll put some monitors on you and give you oxygen. You'll get medicine to relax you, and Dr. Evans will give you numbing medicine in the surgical area. Any questions you'd like to ask me?"

"You hear all sorts of stories about anesthesia not working and all kinds of complications. What if something goes wrong?"

"We'll fix it. Don't worry. All you need to do is relax and go to sleep. I expect everything to go smoothly."

"Well, okay, Dr. Chang," she said. "And I have one more question."

"Yes."

"How did you get a Chinese last name when you look… African-American?"

Sydney stared at her. The surgeon, Dr. Gary Evans, walked in.

"Hello, Margaret. How are you? Is Dr. Chang taking good care of you?"

"Oh, yes."

Evans smirked. "Have a nice sleep, Margaret. I'll see you when it's all over."

Sydney walked over to him and whispered. "You aren't still using Dextran solution, are you?"

"Yes. That's exactly what I'm using, Sydney."

Sydney inhaled through her nose. *Of course he is. Other solutions have less complications.* She placed the monitors on Mrs. Merriweather and gave her extra oxygen by positioning a nasal cannula into her nose. Sydney began an IV.

"I just gave you some medicine that will make you sleepy. Have pleasant dreams."

Through this IV line, Sydney gave her a drug cocktail including an infusion of propofol for hypnosis. The patient fell asleep and breathed rhythmically. Her blood pressure and heart rate were stable.

The nurses positioned, prepped, and draped the patient. After scrubbing and donning his sterile gown and gloves, Dr. Evans injected a local anesthetic, lidocaine, and inserted the hysteroscope.

Eight minutes later, Sydney heard it—the subtle tonal change in the beeping sound and an increase in Mrs. Merriweather's heart rate. She rose, stood over the patient, and cycled the blood pressure cuff. Then she saw it—a deep red spot on the patient's neck. Seconds later, a rash erupted all over her chest, then covered her body. Her heart rate zoomed to 130 beats/minute, her breathing became rapid and shallow with audible wheezing, her oxygen saturation decreased, and her blood pressure dropped.

"Abort the procedure right now, Evans," Sydney said.

She was outwardly calm, with laser focus; her hands moved rapidly. Sydney pushed in epinephrine and Benadryl intravenously, intubated Mrs. Merriweather, and continued ventilation with 100 percent oxygen. She discontinued all anesthetic medication. Twenty seconds later, Mrs. Merriweather's heart stopped. She was in pulseless electrical activity—an electrical rhythm on the electrocardiogram, but no pulse or blood pressure in the patient.

"Start chest compressions," she ordered a nurse. "She's having an allergic reaction to something—probably the Dextran solution. Get the code cart and hit the arrest button." With furrowed brows, Sydney injected more epinephrine, hydrocortisone, and ranitidine into the IV line. "Put the defibrillator pacing pads on."

The OR flooded with help—two more anesthesiologists, two surgeons, and four nurses circled the patient's bed.

Hasina ran in and whispered, "Sydney…"

"Not now. The patient's coding."

Six

"SHE'S GONNA DIE," Dr. Evans said, standing in the corner, shaking his head. He paced to another corner. "She looks terrible; she's gonna die."

"Not helpful," Sydney barked. "Tracy, start an arterial line. Send cardiac arrest blood work and include a tryptase level. Give me a central line kit. George, push another amp of epinephrine. Bob, take over chest compressions from Paula."

"But it looks like she's gonna die," Evans said again.

"She'll survive even if I have to transplant your heart into her. Now shut up—we're actually working," Sydney growled.

Seven minutes later, from red to dead and back, the patient had a pulse—a weak but palpable pulse. They stopped the chest compressions. Twelve minutes later, her oxygenation improved, her wheezing subsided, and her vital signs were stable.

"Good job, you guys. Thanks," Sydney said, exhaling. She shook her head and rolled her eyes. "Get the transport monitors. Let's take her intubated to the ICU."

"What else can I do to help, Sydney?" Bob asked.

"Fire Evans," she muttered.

Dr. Robert Inger, one of the most esteemed surgeons at the hospital, chuckled, "Well, other than that, Sydney?" he said as he removed his face mask, wrapped his gum in it, and tossed it into a garbage can. "By the way, are you around the next few days? I have a couple of big cases coming up and I'd like you to work with me. I'm not sure when, but if you don't mind, I'll request you."

"No problem—just let the scheduling desk know."

Evans stared at his feet and exited.

After Sydney transported Mrs. Merriweather to the ICU and made sure she was properly signed over to the ICU medical staff, she paged Hasina.

"Found Robbie?"

"No!" Hasina wailed.

"Did you call security? Did they close all the exits?"

"Yes and yes."

"Are they calling the cops?"

"Yes."

"They checked the tunnels?"

"I'm not sure."

"I'm going to the tunnels. Then I'll go to the basement and subbasement. When you talk to security, ask them if they've checked those places."

"What about your cases?" Hasina asked.

"I'll get Karen to cover. I'll page you when I come back up."

"Why did I come in for Marlene's case? I didn't have to. Someone else could have done it. It wasn't a complicated one. Why didn't I just say no, Sydney? Why?"

"Because you're always the first one to do a favor."

The skin on Sydney's cheeks burned. She knew they needed to find him now. *What was Hasina thinking when she let him walk alone in this massive hospital at six forty-five A.M.? Stay present. Positive.* Her eyes formed a thin line.

Seven

SYDNEY BOLTED DOWN the stairs. They were her gym at work when she was on call. She knew which ones reentered floors and which ones locked you in. The stairwells were a bleak space with black, well-worn stone steps, grooved with uneven foot impressions. A rounded metal handrail aided those in need of stabilization. Sydney sprinted down and could point out which landings had scrunched beer cans, used joints, and discarded condoms without even seeing them.

Manhattan Hospital was always under construction. It was a city unto itself, a daily host to thousands of people from all walks of life in every imaginable emotional and physical condition. Today, Sydney zeroed in on the desolate stairwells, the ones where a scream had the same volume as a tree falling in an empty forest.

She emerged on the basement level of the Issacs Building, across from the communications office, and dashed in. The woman who broadcast the public address announcements was at the front desk. A few years back, she'd worked in Sydney's department.

"Marilyn, hi. Dr. Wagner's son is missing. Probably just wandered off. Can you please announce his name over the PA system? Direct him to return to Dr. Wagner's office."

"We already put out a Code Pink on him, Dr. Chang. It doesn't go over the PA system, but security has been alerted and all the doors that lock are locked."

"It wasn't announced?"

"Not overhead. A strobe light comes on in the specific area where he was last seen to alert security, but no overhead announcement."

"But would you make an announcement anyway? He might just be playing in an OR. If he hears his name, he'll get a move on."

"Dr. Chang. If it were up to me, I'd do it this second, but I'm not allowed to put anything over the loudspeaker without the proper authority."

"He's been missing for over two hours. Try to get that permission."

Sydney sped into the corridor, popped back into the stairwell, and ran down to the subbasement. She sprinted the equivalent of two city blocks through a windowless dungeon-like tunnel with low ceilings and funky two-toned green walls. She flashed on Harry Moss, her old coach. She hadn't been down there since he'd passed away.

"Robbie!" *He's probably just hiding like I did when I was eight and my parents took me to Sears. I loved reading my books under those racks of long dresses. I didn't resurface until my name was called out over the loudspeaker. Maybe he's just waiting too.*

The hospital underground was complex and confusing, but Sydney was familiar with it because on quiet on-call weekends, she'd go down for a few card games with the staff. Jimmy, a security guard and fellow blackjack player, took her on a tour once and explained the entire layout. The main hospital building connected to four other buildings—resident and medical student housing, an apartment-hotel, and an adjacent hospital. The hospital-to-hospital connecting tunnel required multiple keys to unlock the gates, with video cameras and a buzzer alarm monitored by the security of both institutions. It was unlikely that someone would choose to exit the hospital from one of these areas—too complicated and risky—but there was one exception. The tunnel to the Carson Building had an extra exit that opened onto the street; it required a key to enter but allowed anyone to exit from a stairwell across the street. If someone took Robbie and knew about the tunnels, it was the best way out.

"Robbie! Robbie?" she shouted, flying through the sub-basement with darting eyes and her head swinging like a pendulum. Beads of perspiration dripped down her forehead, her pulse increasing with each deserted hallway.

She entered a site cordoned off by a plastic drape. She pulled it back; the area was stuffed with old hospital equipment and emitted a metallic aroma. The still air was thick and heavy. Dust blanketed discarded, dented stainless steel cabinets and rusted metal machinery. She squeezed into sliver-sized air pockets around and over the equipment. "Robbie, buddy, are you here?" She walked through the medical student tunnel. Security was absent as were any signs of human activity. "Robbie?" The resident tunnel was empty too. So was the hotel tunnel. "Robbie?" *Is he in one of the mechanical rooms downstairs? He loves that stuff.*

She jumped down an isolated stairwell and descended even lower, into the dimmer and bleaker sub-subbasement. Underwhelmed by the steamy heat and earsplitting clank of machines turning on and off every few seconds, she hunted.

Her volume rose. "ROBBIE!"

This area was the size of a professional basketball court. Lightless hidden spots and shadowy areas surrounded sweaty piping that supplied water and steam to the hospital. Sydney squeezed in. Deep in the middle of the room, she heard a shoe shuffle. She tensed, pivoted, and placed her right foot back. She was sideways, in a fighting stance, when a man stepped out from behind a stainless steel steam machine. She inhaled. He was tall, broad, and dark-skinned; it was difficult for her to see anything more than his outline. He approached. Sydney zeroed in on his hospital ID badge. Isaiah Jordan.

"Mr. Jordan, have you seen Mr. Decker?" she said. Mr. Decker was a fixture down there for over sixty years. Everybody knew Deck.

"Mr. Decker don't work down here no more. He's up in central sterile now. You don't remember me, do ya, Dr. Chang? You did my wife's epidural a few years back."

"Right. Right. You're Grace's husband."

"Guilty. Everything okay, Doc? What brings you to the sub-sub?"

"I'm looking for a little boy who's missing. Have you seen him? He's about seven, blond, blue eyes."

"No, but I'll keep a lookout. Don't worry. No funny business goes on during my shift."

"If you see anything odd or see him, please call hospital security ASAP. Everyone's looking for him."

Eight

"Thanks for running down your morning for me, Doctor," said Detective Thomas as his dark brown, almost black, eyes darted around her office. There were two framed photos of Robbie on her desk; one of him alone, the other of the two of them. A poster-sized frog painting with Robbie's bold and curly signature hung on the wall across from her desk.

"Pretty fond of that little guy, aren't ya?" the detective asked, his voice a bass baritone.

"Yes." She took a sip from her cobalt-blue water bottle.

"How is it that you two became so close?"

"Hasina—Dr. Wagner—invited me over for dinner about two years ago, and Robbie and I hit it off. We hang out on Sundays."

"Oh, so you saw him yesterday?"

"No, during the summer their family goes on outings. I haven't seen Robbie for about three weeks."

"I bet you miss him."

"I do."

"So, what do you do on Sundays when Robbie's not around?"

"Skate."

"I see. Are you friendly with Dr. Wagner's other children?"

"Just Robbie."

"How long have you had this, um, relationship with him?"

Relationship? He makes it sound sinister. "Since he was five."

"Do you usually make friends with people Robbie's age, Doctor?"

Sydney stared at his piano-straight teeth, bright white compared to his chestnut complexion. "No." *What an ass.*

"Uh-huh. Just hit it off, then?"

"Yes."

"Are ya married?"

Sydney frowned at him and shook her head slowly.

"The hospital video shows Robbie leaving the building. Can you think of any reason why he'd leave the hospital on his own and from the side entrance?"

"He left the hospital?" Her head tilted sideways, her chin jutted down, and her forehead furrowed. "Which door?"

"Eighty-Second Street. Do you know why he'd leave?"

"He probably decided to meet me outside."

"But how would he know where you'd be entering? There are five entrances to this hospital, aren't there?"

"There are at least ten, but Hasina parks at that entrance. A few times she's had Robbie with her, and he saw me skate up in the morning. He knows that's where I enter."

"You always enter from the same place?"

"Yes. Did you see which way he went?" Sydney asked.

"He was standing by the curb."

"And then where did he go?"

"How would you categorize your relationship with Robbie? Big sister/little brother, aunt/nephew, motherly?"

Her eyes fixed on his. "Don't be tedious, Detective. We're friends."

"Friends?"

"Yes."

"There's a big age difference, is all."

Sydney stared down at her hands, resisting the urge to bash his head into the wall. She shifted in her seat.

Her office door swung open. In walked a blue-eyed man with wavy salt-and-pepper hair, narrow-cut black slacks, and saddle-colored Oxfords. He wore a lab coat so crisp, it looked like it could stand on its own. He glanced at them, ambled to the door on the other side of the room, opened it, and Sydney's office flooded with sunlight.

"Detective Thomas, this is Dr. Charles Lansing, another anesthesiologist. I already asked him if he saw Robbie this morning," Sydney said.

Detective Thomas stood and walked over to Dr. Lansing, dwarfing him. The detective extended his hand.

"I didn't see him; I didn't get here until just after eight this morning," Lansing said with a British accent, shaking the detective's hand. The accent always amused Sydney because Lansing had left London when he was two and grown up on Long Island, New York.

"Will you be available to speak with me in a few minutes?" Thomas asked.

"Sure. Just knock," he said as he entered his office and closed the door.

"How long have the two of you been in this office space?"

"Two years for me. One for him. I was an attending for a year, and then when he finished his residency, he moved in."

"So he walks through yours all day long?"

"Yes."

"Anything else you want to tell me, Doctor?"

"Don't forget to check the hospital tunnels. I looked down there already, but your people should check them again."

"My guys are there now. Please give me your cell number in case I need to contact you."

"I don't have one."

"You're kidding."

"You can reach me at home or the office. Or by beeper, but it only works close to the hospital." She scribbled her numbers on a loose piece of paper.

Detective Thomas clipped the paper to his notebook, clicked off his phone video, and stood. He studied Sydney a beat longer than necessary, then knocked on Charles's door.

Nine

On her way to the OR, Sydney noticed two men with thick dark hair and black suits standing off in a corner whispering. Badges that looked like backstage passes dangled down their chests. *Definitely FBI.* She popped into an unoccupied OR, picked up the phone, and dialed.

"Hullo," Lily muttered.

"Are you coherent?" Sydney asked since she assumed that Lily was still in bed, judging from her voice and the static on the old Princess phone connection. It was the original phone that their father had surprised Lily with on her thirteenth birthday; it sat on her bedside table.

"Yeah."

"No more, Lily."

"No more what?"

"Rescue. Cleanup."

Lily grunted. "Well, you don't have to do anything. I never asked you to find me. Ever."

"Lily, you were doing so well."

No response.

"Lily?"

"I have issues," Lily whispered.

"Everyone has issues. Suck it up like the rest of us," Sydney said in a controlled voice.

"Yeah, well, it's easy for you to say, Sydney. Everything has always worked out for you. For me, nothing ever works out."

"I can't do this now. If things calm down by the weekend, we can talk on Saturday."

"I'm busy."

"Make yourself unbusy. And your handbag is on the doorknob."

Their father, a prominent doctor in Chinatown, kept an array of medicines on hand in case he needed to make an emergency house call, and Sydney knew that her sister pinched a pill here and there. Back at her desk, she flashed on the night Lily sat with her chin buried into her chest. Chinese delicacies covered the round teak dining table, as usual, but no one was eating. Sydney piped up, blaming Lily's erratic behavior and sleepiness on food poisoning from the bad pickles in the school cafeteria. "I'm feeling queasy too. Reaaaal queasy." Lily's drug use kicked into high gear when their father died two years later.

Ten

Hasina was in the outer office where the secretaries sat. She clutched an enlarged recent photo of Robbie and was shuffling back and forth, creating a breeze as she worked all three copying machines. His smiling face was shooting out in two-second intervals. She stacked them into piles, the back of her hand wiping the streams of moisture off of her fleshy neck.

"Haven't the police already made flyers and posted them all over?" Sydney asked.

"The detective just informed me that the administration does not consider this a hospital problem since Robbie was last seen on the street and exited on his own free will."

"Of course they're making this an outside problem." Sydney felt her throat tighten. She turned away and inhaled two slow, deep breaths through her nostrils.

"Here, please help me hand these out, Sydney," Hasina said and thrust a huge stack into her hands.

Sydney was on the fifth floor, distributing flyers to a group standing around a coffee machine, when a serious looking redheaded man with a pointy nose approached.

"Excuse me, you are?" he said as he picked up his pace behind her.

"And you are?" she replied without turning around.

"Hank Johnson, COO. And you are, again?"

She swung around, held out her badge, and pivoted back.

"One minute, Dr. Chang."

She stopped, her back to his face.

"What are you handing out?"

"Not your concern."

"I think it is. This is hospital property."

"This is a nonprofit organization, Mr. Johnson." She turned to face him. "An organization that is partially floated by the government, which means us, the taxpayers. I can hand out personal notes to my friends whenever and wherever I like."

"And all of these people are your friends?"

"They certainly are."

"I need you to stop distributing that on hospital property."

"Really?" she said into his ear in a soft voice as she dipped into his personal space and continued walking. Within seconds, an old familiar sensation returned—an instantaneous flame of wild fury lit deep within her gut. The heat worked its way up the back of her neck and into her scalp, her eyes enlarged, and the rage that she stifled and struggled to keep in check reignited.

Rounding the corner, she saw him pull out his cell phone.

Handing a few flyers to every person, she moved on to each floor until she completed one building, then started on the next. When all three hundred were dispersed, she climbed the steps, two at a time, back to Hasina's office.

"Give me more. I'll post them in the neighborhood. I got out of the OR for the rest of the day."

"My secretary's high school son is coming over with his classmates. They'll be here in five minutes. They're going to flyer the whole Upper East Side, working from the hospital out," Hasina said as she lumbered between machines.

"Martyn and the kids just arrived. He called me from the parking garage in our building. The FBI is driving me there; they want us to wait and see if we get a ransom call. A ransom call! Dear God." She gasped.

"Don't let the kids out of your sight or Martyn's. You don't know if this is personal."

"What? Personal? Who would have anything against us?"

"Just be careful. Call me if I can be of any help."

"I'm dying, Sydney."

"Stay strong. You have to for Robbie and the boys."

Hasina's beeper blared. "The FBI wants me to look at a car they flagged."

Eleven

ADRENALINE SURGED THROUGH Sydney's body as she skated out the Eighty-Second Street exit past the curb where Robbie was last seen. It was a tiny and hectic entrance—a small bay area with a couple of parked ambulances and two sanitation Dumpsters, room for two or three cars to drop off and pick up, and a row of waist-high evergreen shrubs. Patients can't enter; the door was ID key locked. But anyone can exit. There was a camera, but no human. The only new edition was a long white van with an intricate rooftop antenna. It sat idling in front of a fire hydrant. Sydney's beeper vibrated.

> Dr. Verdi wants to talk to you in the chairman's suite ASAP.

Ignoring it, she placed the beeper in her pocket.

Like a released caged animal, she bent over, swung her arms, and pushed her legs forward into impossible evening rush-hour traffic. Cars, taxis, bicyclists, and aggressive women pushing expensive baby carriages the size of mini SUVs darted in front of, behind, and around her. Sydney weaved through. *Was he taken randomly? A crime of opportunity? Who would have taken him? Is it tied into the hospital in some way? What about when the FBI came here last year and removed a computer from an OR because it supposedly had kiddie porn on it? They shut down three ORs that day.*

She skated downtown, west to the Apple store on Fourteenth Street and Ninth Avenue. After purchasing an iPad with cash, she headed over to Starbucks on Astor Place.

In leggings and a white T-shirt, Sydney blended in with purple-haired artists, NYU students, and the after-work crowd, amped on espresso. She found a seat in the back, checked for bedbugs, and, with a venti iced Americano, settled in.

She plugged "kidnapping," "pedophilia," and "human trafficking" into DuckDuckGo, an untraceable search engine, and screen after screen of missing children's photos appeared. It confirmed the insidious and uncontrolled nightmare of human trafficking both internationally and locally.

The most important piece of information, she already knew.

TIME IS OF THE ESSENCE. The first four hours after a child goes missing are critical. If not found within these first few hours, the chances of finding them alive fall precipitously.

The first four hours are over. Let the authorities do their work. Stay calm. They'll find him. They have the most resources. Trust them to do their job.

Reading on, she noted that the next most important period was the first forty-eight hours, which was now. The actions of the parents and law enforcement were vital to the recovery of the missing child. BOLOs ("Be on the Lookout" bulletins) and the NCIC (National Crime Information Center) inform a whole swath of law enforcement agencies about missing people and criminal activity. But "after forty-eight," as they refer to it at the forty-ninth hour, a missing person's case operated more on hope than action. *It won't get to that.*

She found the Gosch case. He was a cute blond, blue-eyed twelve-year-old abducted while working his newspaper route in his small Iowa neighborhood early one morning. From the reports Sydney read, it seemed like the police, judges, and politicians across several connecting states were intertwined with a pedophilic ring that operated throughout a sizable expanse of the Midwest. His mother claimed that a large and expensive cover-up ensued. The Gosch boy was never found and no one was prosecuted. Sydney's head pounded.

She read about NAMBLA, North American Man/Boy Love Association, and how its thousands of adult male members believe that it's acceptable to have sex with minors. Her left leg jiggled. She perused case after case of young children's abductions with bad outcomes. She read about online groups where wealthy male pedophiles put in their specifications for the exact type of child they desired. If they bid for a child that a group already possessed, it was cheaper than if they had to special order one. Blond-haired, blue-eyed boys were the most expensive.

Three hours later, she stopped. *With Robbie, it's different. This wasn't a dirt road in a deserted woodsy area where a kid walked home alone from a bus stop. Who knew that Robbie would be in that spot at that time? Not even Hasina. He'd never go off willingly with a stranger. So if it was random, how was he taken so quietly?*

She wiped down the table and chair to erase any fingerprints in case she was being watched and followed. At ten P.M., Sydney placed a key in her apartment door, and unlike usual, she let it slam shut. The indicator light from the phone machine in the kitchen blinked a soft red hue into the foyer. She turned the corner and looked. *One.* One new message. Her heart leapt. "Tuesday, nine fourteen P.M. 'Hey, baby, it's Mick. Are we still on for—'" Sydney pressed stop.

Her fist hit the wall. "Fuck!" *Who lets a little kid walk through deserted hallways alone?* Boom. Boom. Pummeling the wall, she found a rhythm. *Fucking Moron.* Red spots dotted the white wall. She eyed her swelling knuckles. Bang. *Is he alive? Hurt?* When her knuckles were numb and bloodied, she dropped her hands, hung her head, and took a jagged breath. Goose bumps speckled her bare arms and legs.

Sydney got a soapy washcloth and cleaned the wall, iced her knuckles for ten minutes, and made a cup of tea. Sitting on a card chair, she bit the ends off of a red licorice twist and sucked the hot chamomile tea through it.

Two hours in, I thought he was hiding. Four hours later, I was sure that the FBI and police would find him. It's been seventeen hours. He really is gone.

Twelve

A JARRING SOUND jolted her. The open book on her chest crashed to the ground. The clock on the side table read five A.M. She rubbed her eyes and the phone rang again. *Maybe they found him.* She leapt out of the lounge chair. *Ow!* She landed on the side of her foot, and her lower left leg knotted into a spasm. Wincing, she hopped over to the kitchen.

"Hello," she said with squinted eyes.

"Syd. Lily's gone."

"Ma," she said.

"She left yesterday around noon and never came back."

"Lily's back to her old ways. She'll surface. I can't do anything about it now. If you haven't heard from her by five tonight, call me."

"Crap!" she bellowed after she banged the receiver into the cradle. She dropped to the ground, massaged her leg, and inhaled with closed eyes. When she stood, her thumb hit play on her answering machine.

"—tonight. I thought tonight was a go, sexy? Okay, call my cell. Have you forgotten me, baby? Well, it's after nine and I'm taking myself to dinner; wish it was with you. Anyway...if you free up, call me."

Sydney scrunched her face. Sydney and Mick had seen each other every Tuesday evening for the past eight months. He was a smart, rugged, and sweet international photojournalist who yearned for more. Tuesday evenings were all Sydney gave him. *He'll get over it. Or not.*

Thirteen

THE SUBBASEMENT'S AIR was dense, damp, and greasy. Sydney's lungs constricted. She limped through the oppressive hallways in search of Smikes, the head of the PPA pool. To Smikes and his crew, it was a second home. They spent the majority of their time in offices, patients' rooms, and ORs, but at the beginning and end of each day, the sub was where they drank their coffee, ate their food, and caught up on recent news. It's where they donated money to Girl Scout cookie drives, shared family recipes, and comforted one another when they lost loved ones. It was far from pretty, but it was theirs.

Sydney's rubber soles scrunched along the oily linoleum floor in concert with the noisy footfalls of the staff who passed by with warm smiles and nods. It was in sharp contrast to the floors above, where they moved silently over smooth, shiny marble floors with downward gazes.

On this turf, her thoughts moved to Harry Moss again. Along with being a PPA in the OR, he had been Sydney's teacher. Her tennis teacher. Every Saturday and Sunday morning at five thirty, they had practiced on the roof of the hospital, until that one morning when he didn't show. "Good Morning,

Dr. Chang" startled her. It was Grace Jordan, the slim, quiet woman who cleaned the offices on her floor.

"Please call me Sydney. Remember we dropped the last-name thing? Have you seen Smikes?"

"No. If I do, I'll tell him you're looking for him. All right, now," Grace said as she pushed her loaded cart down the hall.

Sydney searched every hallway as workers dashed in and out of locker rooms, changed into blue uniforms, and packed their carts with bleach, ammonia, and towels. She spotted an elderly PPA hunched over filling a cup at the water cooler.

"Hey, Louis, how's your back? Looks like you're standing straighter."

"Can't complain." He beamed.

"I'm looking for Smikes."

"Just went into the men's room."

Sydney turned the corner and found the restroom. She waited across the hall. Otis, a fellow card player with a huge grin, walked up and gave her a high five.

"Hey, Otis."

"I gotta say, it's a bit too early for a card game *now*." He laughed.

Sydney made a best-effort smile. "Not today."

"You be cool, Doc."

When Sydney was first hired, the upstairs personnel had given her a mixed welcome, while the downstairs crew, well, their eyes shone with pride. She was invited to their weddings and christenings, and every week, without fail, someone fed her. Women and men lugged in plastic Tupperware containers from Brooklyn, Queens, and the Bronx packed with curried goat, oxtail, and glazed sweet potatoes. They learned what she liked, and they made sure that *their* doctor got it. Christmas was a bonanza with Elsie's fruitcake, Macie's peppermint candy, and Leroy's all-butter pound cake—there was nothing like Leroy's pound cake.

When someone from housekeeping or the PPA pool needed an operation or had a loved one who did, they requested Dr. Chang and only Dr. Chang. She didn't attend their weddings, but she always rearranged her schedule to personally take care of any request from the staff.

Smikes, a pint-sized, wiry, brown-skinned man with an easy smile and a tightly cropped Afro, exited the bathroom. At fifty-one, he was muscled with a rock-hard physique and a no-nonsense attitude—a tough, but likable boss.

"Have a moment?" Sydney said.

"Sure, Doc. Been a while. Okay." Leaning his left shoulder on the wall, he looked straight into her eyes. Sydney drew in close.

"I need your help. I'd like a list of everyone who worked the Tuesday twelve to seven A.M. shift separated by building," she said in a hushed tone.

"Uh, well. You know, I'm not supposed to give that out. What's going on?" he asked, narrowing his eyes and cocking his head.

"It's personal, Smikes."

"Does this have anything to do with that little boy who went missing? You don't think any of my people were involved, now do you?" He moved in close with a fixed stare.

"I don't. But that little boy is like family to me."

"Wasn't he a little blond boy?"

"Yes."

"Gee, Doc. I didn't realize. I'm sorry. Wow."

"So I'd appreciate it if somehow that material ended up in my hands."

"Let me just say again, I know my staff. I can tell you it's not one of my guys." His eyebrows arched, his lips pressed together, and his head shook. "Not one of my guys."

"I just want to find out if they saw anything, that's all. And, oh, since it's a change of shift, would you round up as many people as possible right now so I can speak to them?"

"Meet me in the coffee room in ten minutes. How's that?"

"Perfect. Thanks, Smikes."

He tapped her gently on the back and strode away with his characteristic side bounce.

Minutes later, Sydney was positioned by the open door of the "break" room, a square, antiseptic space. Inside, an ancient and discolored drip coffee machine sat on a card table, along with some plastic spoons, a carton of milk, and a half-eaten homemade carrot cake. A plastic knife and napkins were off to the side. A sea of azure-uniformed staff ranging in age from early twenties to late sixties stood waiting. The group was split fifty–fifty between men and women, and their skin tones ran the gamut from alabaster to ebony. They were tall and short, skinny and stout, and everything in between.

The space held fifteen adults comfortably, but within minutes, around thirty additional people crammed in, with another ten or so splayed out into the hallway. This was only a fraction of the staff, since most were either off duty or already on the floors. Sydney considered it a good start. She knew how quickly word spread, and if she made a good pitch, she was confident that her message would be all over the hospital within the hour.

She wove in and out on her way to the blackboard up front. With her back to the group, she wrote her name and beeper number. As she scribbled, she caught pieces of whispered conversations.

"She played tennis with Harry," one woman said.

"What did he have again, a heart attack or somethin'?" another asked.

"Asthma. Come over him just like that."

"They was such good friends."

Sydney's eyes glazed, and she thought of Robbie. *"Mommy told me that your friend died. I know you're sad. I know you love coffee. I have a quarter."*

"Halle Berry got nothing on her, tell ya that much." A few men chuckled.

"But she's light. I think she got some mix in her. Last name is Chinese," a female voice said.

Sydney turned around with a tight smile and nodded. They returned it. She looked out at the group.

From the sidelines two male PPAs spoke in not-so-hushed tones. "Yeah, I know, Dr. Chang. She cool. Fiiiiine, too."

"Man, you need to stop." His friend laughed. Sydney heard this exchange and looked down at her feet. Once or twice a month, she received notes under her door with polite requests for dates.

Smikes walked in. He raised his hands way above his head. "Everybody, good morning. I'm sure a lot of you know Dr. Chang. And if you don't know her personally, then I'm sure you know *of* her. Please give her your attention—there's something important she needs to discuss with us." He looked at Sydney. "Doctor," he said.

"I see a lot of familiar faces in the crowd. In fact, I've known some of you since I started here six years ago. It's good to see you all. I'm here to ask a favor. The child on the flyer that's been circulating, the little blond boy, the one who went missing from in front of the hospital yesterday, is a friend of mine. He's Dr. Wagner's son, and his name's Robbie. As you know, every minute counts in a missing child's case. I know you folks see and hear it all; you catch everything. No matter how insignificant you may think something is, go to the police or come to me if you're not comfortable going to them. My beeper number is on the board. Any intuition or bad feelings, anything that occurred that might be different from the regular routine, please call. Any stranger who you may have seen that seemed weird or out of place... You never know how meaningful, how important something is until you add it all up. Also, please pass this message along to all of your friends in the hospital. The more people who are aware, the better chance we have of finding Robbie. So please spread the news."

A deep male voice yelled from the back, "Not for nothing, Doc, but we can't jeopardize our jobs now. You can understand that."

"I do. And I respect that. You can slip an anonymous message into my locked mailbox in the hallway outside of my office; it has my name on it. I'll be discreet. I know what you're up against."

Most heads nodded yes. Some stared blankly with sad eyes.

"Dr. Chang has been a friend for a long time. I'm going to do the best I can to help her. I hope y'all will too," Smikes interjected.

"What's the little guy's full name, Dr. Chang?" an older woman called out from the hallway.

"Robbie Wagner."

"Okay, y'all, let's get back to work. Anyone have any information about Robbie, let Dr. Chang or me know. Thanks," Smikes said and waved his hands sideways toward the open door.

Sydney raised her hand up high and nodded. As she turned to leave, an older male voice spoke out. "Be careful, Doc; this hospital ain't safe late at night. And this is for all of y'all to hear too. Just last week, a weekend night, I was workin' the fourteenth floor and around one A.M. I seen this man who I never seen before walk into an OR, and when I looked in, he was putting syringes in his jacket pocket. Never know what goes on in here."

"Thanks a lot, Smikes; you're the best," she said.

"I'll be in touch about the other thing."

"I appreciate it. How's your new granddaughter?" she asked.
"God bless, she's adorable."

Sydney looped around the long corridor and entered the telecom room. Marilyn was at the desk again.

"Any chance you can print out a list of all of the attendings and administrators who worked two nights ago?"

"I'm so sorry, but I just can't. Once again, I'm not at liberty…"

"Okay, Marilyn. Thanks anyway."

Down the hall, Sydney opened the door to the stairwell. The climb up felt like the meaty part of her lower left leg was locked in a metal clamp, and it got tighter and tighter with each step. Usually, movement loosened it up.

Sydney only made it to the fourth floor. She entered a corridor bustling with activity. Men and women in dark suits stood around talking into neckpieces, monitoring two long lines filled with nurses, hospital staff, and a few attending physicians.

"What's going on?" Sydney asked one of the suits.

"The hospital staff is being questioned about the missing child."

"FBI?"

"Yes."

Sydney limped by an open anteroom, noticing that one queue led to a bank of tables with a stern-looking middle-aged woman sitting at a computer, and the other led to the front of a closed metal door at the rear of the room.

Fourteen

"They're contacting my family in Egypt, like it's terrorist-related. But the hospital is not involved; does that make sense?" Hasina said.

Sydney paced with the phone pressed against her ear.

"All they know is that when he walked out of the building, he was talking to a blond woman and a young boy. He walked to the curb with them, and then the bushes blocked the view," Hasina said.

"What were they actually able to see?" Sydney sat back down. She tucked the phone in the crook of her neck and noticed that her index finger was bleeding.

"Cars came and went. The woman was bent over talking, probably to Robbie. Then she got into one of the waiting cars. They can't identify the license plate."

Sydney froze. "Did Robbie get in too?"

"They couldn't see through the bushes! I told you that. Sydney, are you with me?"

"And they cleared all of the other cars?" Sydney asked with a tight voice.

"Yes. They saw this car on camera going up the FDR to the Willis Ave. Bridge. Then the cameras cut off. I've got to go! Martyn is waving at me to hang up."

Sydney stamped her foot.

"One second. Were they tracked through the building?"

Hasina blew her nose. "The woman entered the building with the boy around eleven P.M. They sat in patient areas and used the bathrooms on several floors. No fingerprint information. They entered the old med school building around two A.M. and then they lost them. It's not camera-ed up. The next time they were seen was when they left the hospital with Robbie."

"Any ransom demands?"

"No." Hasina sobbed.

"Do you want me to come by and search?"

"No. Seventy-five people are out looking. Martyn and the boys made routes."

"The boys are out searching?"

"Yes."

"Uh-huh."

Sydney dropped to the floor and cranked out push-ups. Forty-eight, forty-nine, fifty. Stomach crunches. One hundred... one hundred and ten.

"This is Sydney Chang, Lily Chang's sister. We have a family emergency and I need to reach Lily." She was on the phone to the Manhattan School of Mortuary Services. "Could you locate her for me, please?"

"Let me check the computer. One moment. Okay, hmm, Lily hasn't swiped in this morning," the receptionist said.

"Could you tell me what time she checked out of school yesterday?" Sydney asked.

"I'm sorry. I'm not able to give out that kind of information."

"It's an emergency; I need to get in touch with her as soon as possible."

"I'll be happy to tell her you called, Ms. Chang, if I see her."

Sydney hung up and kicked the garbage can underneath her desk.

Fifteen

"THAT'S HER. I told you you'd know who she was," a plump housekeeper whispered to her associate as they strolled past. A dark-skinned older man, part of the OR cleaning staff, nodded at Sydney as she continued down the corridor.

Sydney avoided eye contact. She walked straight to her computer and reviewed the stats of the upcoming case, blocking out the incessant background chatter. Only a handful of nurses knew of Sydney's close connection to the missing boy. None of them were in the room this morning.

"Who would have thought a child could be abducted from a hospital? It's scary," said Jessie, a blond, perky nurse and single mother in her midthirties.

"Yeah. A hospital? Don't people think of hospitals in a sacred way, like churches or something?" asked Carol, a dark-haired, skinny nurse and mother of two. Sydney nodded.

"I know my family and friends think you go to a hospital to be saved—not kidnapped!" added Latoya, a petite, married nurse in her early thirties, clanking her instruments onto the OR table.

"I would never let my child walk alone in a hospital. Not ever. And at that hour, so early in the morning, when no one was around—what's up with that?" Carol said as she picked up a loaded tray and brought it across the room.

"I'm scared for that little boy. Who knows what's happening to him, who has him, what they're doing to him?" Latoya said. "It's just awful. He may not even be…"

"Enough, ladies. Let's get some work done today," Sydney said.

Their glances fell on one another like a line of tapped dominos. Silence ensued. Tasks resumed.

Sydney tilted her neck left and right, rolled it forward and back, then back and forward as the patient and his mother were escorted into the OR.

First up was a curly-headed six-year-old in need of ear tubes. Routine. She explained her part of the procedure to the apprehensive-looking parent and to little Tyler. She smiled as she looked into his cute brown eyes. After the mask was placed on his face and he fell asleep, his mom left. Fifteen minutes later, the surgeon completed the operation. Sydney carried Tyler into the recovery room and placed him into his mother's waiting arms.

Between patients, the PPAs cleaned and disinfected the operating room as the nurses finished their paperwork and readied the equipment for the next case. The conversation continued behind Sydney's back as she reset the anesthetic medications for the next case, a gallbladder removal in a fifty-three-year-old woman.

"A lot of bad stuff goes on in the hospital that no one ever finds out about," Jesse said.

"Yeah. That's because the administration keeps a lid on it. Just like the church does," Carol replied.

"Come on, now, Carol. Don't go bad-mouthing the church. What's your problem with the church today?" Latoya asked.

"Remember when that sweet medical student—what was her name, Nancy? Nan? Something with an *N*—well, remember when she was raped in the stairwell? By a security guard!" Carol said. "Did the administration do anything about it? No. They fired the guy but kept it quiet and squashed it like it never happened. No press. The church did the same thing for their priests—for years, they looked the other way. All I'm saying is when the 'powers that be' want it quiet, it doesn't matter what happens or where you are, it's kept quiet," Carol said.

"Well, do you think administration is keeping a lid on this missing-boy case?" Jesse asked.

"No comment," Carol replied. "But they don't want people to think you can bring your child to a hospital, and if you don't watch them carefully, they can be stolen like at a supermarket. Remember a few years back, when Dr. Banks was accused of molesting patients? Did that make the news? No."

"Really?" Jesse asked. "I didn't know that."

"You weren't here. But, Dr. Chang, you must remember that?" Carol asked.

"Quiet, the patient's about to enter," Sydney said, and her beeper zinged.

> Dr. Roth is coming to relieve you. Please be in my office in five minutes. Anthony.

Sixteen

"AVE A SEAT, Sydney," said Dr. Anthony Verdi, the chief of anesthesiology.

"I'll stand, thanks."

Verdi, the chief for the past three years, was in his early fifties, a six-footer with straight, yellow-hued teeth and brushed-back hair. A gaudy star sapphire ring set in gold adorned his left pink finger on callus-free hands. To say that Sydney and Verdi were cordial would be a gross exaggeration. Tolerant of each other would be closer to the truth.

Sydney nodded to the pointy-nosed, thin-lipped Hank Johnson, seated at Verdi's desk.

"Hank asked you to stop handing out flyers the other day, and we saw some on the floors this morning," Verdi said.

Sydney shrugged and looked into his eyes.

"Frankly, it's not your concern, Sydney, so stay out of it. The authorities are working on it. They've assured us that the problem occurred outside of the hospital. So it's not a hospital problem."

"Don't be ridiculous. It certainly is my concern, and it should be everyone's," she said as she looked at both Verdi and Johnson.

"You don't want this to affect your job, Dr. Chang," Johnson said.

Sydney smiled.

"It's not a hospital problem; no more interfering, Sydney," said Verdi.

On her way out, at the end of the hallway, her right foot shot up four and a half feet and viscously slammed into the silver square pressure pad on the wall. The OR doors parted.

Seventeen

SYDNEY SAT ON her mother's living room couch a few hours later. As usual, the Yankees game was on. The volume blasted with the voices of announcers calling plays as she sank farther into the battered brown leather.

Her mother entered the dim living room carrying a plate piled with juicy slider-sized hamburgers, steamed bok choy, and a buttered baked potato. Sydney moved to the round dining table. Several minutes passed before she looked up.

"Maybe she's just out? Let's give her some time to come home," Sydney said.

"You really think she's just out, after the other night?"

Sydney placed a slice of potato into her mouth. Her mother sat by her side and ate quietly.

Nellie Ping Chang, a Chinese woman who grew up in Fort Erie, Canada, was five feet in heels. At seventy-seven years of age, she was still a regal beauty. Nellie was a gourmet cook, a graduate of Barnard College, and a former professional poker player. She'd settled down at forty-five years old, married a straitlaced Chinese doctor, and adopted Lily and Sydney.

Photos of the family lined the entire top shelf. They started with Lily from age four and Sydney as a baby. The girls were like mismatched bookends. One was a Chinese toddler with a porcelain complexion; the other was a darker-skinned mixed child. Lily's birth parents were Chinese; she came to the Changs from an orphanage at age four. Sydney came the day she was born to a Chinese mother and an African-American father.

Most of the photos were taken when the girls were young. The majority were of Lily and their father on Sunday outings in Chinatown, where he had his medical practice. In one, Lily was about five years old, smiling in a fluffy white dress, with a crooked pink bow in her hair, holding the giant stuffed tiger that her father had just bought her. She was sitting in his lap. In a different shot, Lily was waving from the front seat of their dad's brand-new navy-blue Lincoln Continental. Sydney peered at the roller-skate photo: Lily stood holding up new white skates that their father had surprised her with. Sydney remembered being beyond envious. It wasn't even Lily's birthday or Christmas; he'd just bought them for her. Sydney was never taken to Chinatown. Some Sundays, her mother took her to the Bronx Zoo, where Sydney read every caption and viewed every video while her mother waited patiently.

There were no solos of Sydney, and none with Sydney and their father alone. Sydney's eyes stopped at the photo of her Uncle Wai, in his late thirties, with four-year-old Sydney sitting on his shoulders grinning. "Wai Sook" is what she called her father's brother. Every Friday evening, Sydney and Lily were dropped off at their grandmother's apartment. After hours of her grandmother tugging on Sydney's hair, trying to comb it, they'd all have dinner. Then, Lily would practice the piano for two hours, while Wai Sook, a former marine who'd lost two fingers serving abroad, taught Sydney how to fight. They'd wrestle until nine forty-five exactly, then he'd fill a crystal glass with ice and Hennessy, and they'd settle next to each other to watch his favorite TV mystery. She worked to stay awake, but never managed to see more than the first ten minutes before passing out onto his side. Sydney's eyes smiled. She moved on to a photo of Lily playing the piano. Her dead father's words still echoed in her ears: "You'll take care of your sister. She's so pretty. You're smart."

She swallowed, stuck her fork into the bok choy—her favorite—and twisted it. "I called Lily's school this morning, and they said she wasn't in yet. That was all they'd tell me. Did she go to classes last week?"

"She was out the door by seven every morning."

Her mother flipped the station to the local news.

In the middle of Sydney's third ketchup-drenched burger, an Amber Alert bulletin scrolled across the bottom of the screen.

> NEW YORK AMBER ALERT: Robbie Wagner, seven, missing from East Eighty-Second Street since yesterday morning.

The announcer broke in, "A person of interest is being sought in the disappearance of Robbie Wagner..."

"Wagner? Isn't he the son of the heavyset woman you work with at the hospital?" her mother asked.

"Shush," Sydney said as she stood and moved in front of the television.

"He was last seen talking to an unidentified blond woman as she got into a black Honda Accord with black-tinted rear windows." A grainy close-up photo of a middle-aged blond woman holding the hand of a boy of about ten wearing a baseball cap and black-rimmed glasses, talking to a shorter boy, popped onto the screen. They froze the image. The shorter boy was Robbie. "Anyone with any information is being asked to call: 800-222-8686. A reward is being offered for information leading to the whereabouts of this boy, Robbie Wagner. On a lighter note…"

"Does this have anything to do with the hospital?" her mother asked.

"Yes. Hasina had an early case and took him with her. She let him walk to my office alone. And I wasn't there yet. So I never saw him."

"She let him walk around by himself?"

Sydney was silent.

"You really never know what goes on in someone's home when the door closes," her mother said and sighed. "Anyway, your sister's not home. Go look for her."

Eighteen

HOT, STICKY EVENING air clung to Sydney's skin as she sped to Stuyvesant Park, a few short blocks from her mother's apartment. It used to be a beautiful neighborhood park until Downtown Hospital opened the Zimmer Center for Addiction Treatment. The center, located across the street from the park, was renowned for its methadone program. Monday through Friday, the drug-addled swooped into the area from the five boroughs. Most, like Lily, arrived first thing in the morning, picked up their medications, and left. Others made it a "park" day; they bumped up their meds, exchanged them with friends, or sold them to eager buyers. There were a lot of interested takers. The benches were usually filled with people in various states of consciousness, and Sydney worried that Lily was one of them tonight.

Placed in a nameless part of the city—not quite the East Village, Gramercy, or Union Square—Stuyvesant had a sullied reputation. Situated across from the private school that Lily and Sydney attended from kindergarten through twelfth grade, the park was a virtual candy store for students interested in recreational drugs.

As Sydney approached, she noticed that it was unusually quiet and dark. The gate was barely visible as her open hand pushed on the thick bars. Chains jangled. Nothing moved. She shoved it, and it rattled again. The ten-foot-high metal fence was composed of individually spiked poles approximately four inches apart, encompassing the entire park. Its gaps were too small to squeeze through, even for Lily. Sydney peered in. It looked empty. Odd. She checked her watch: eighteen minutes past eleven. She glanced at a small green sign posted on the side of the gate: PARK CLOSES AT ELEVEN P.M.

Finally, the rule is enforced—one less place to look. She dashed around the perimeter and shook all the gate entrances, then headed uptown. It was going to be a long night, and all she wanted to do was get into bed.

She approached Madison Square Park on Fifth Avenue. Unlike Stuyvesant, the closing time was a joke. A low three-and-a-half-foot-tall fence surrounded the vast border, and people hopped it all night long. There was a padlock on the small main gate. She rolled her eyes and sighed. Strolling to the darkest side of the park on Madison Avenue, she looked left and right, then placed her hands on the waist-high metal fence, and popped over.

Situated diagonally across from the Flatiron Building, it was packed with tourists and amateur photographers during daylight hours. Addicts, runaways, and homeless people entered after midnight. With plenty of hidden spots, it was the perfect place to engage in clandestine activity.

She worked from back to front. "Have you seen a thirty-year-old Asian woman, five four, dressed in black?" she repeated to a series of figures slumped over in the shadows. On rare occasions, her query elicited a grunt. Sometimes she received a slow side-to-side head shake, but more often than not, all she drew was a dull, blank stare, the same faraway, hollow-eyed gaze that Lily wore when she was high.

Sydney's mind traveled back to fourth grade. In their tightly knit private school, the grades overlapped in gym class. Lily was everyone's first pick—the golden girl. Considered the best female athlete at the school in soccer, basketball, and baseball, she was lean, strong, and shrewd. Lily agreed to be on someone's team only after she whispered into their leader's ear. Each one nodded, grimaced, and picked Sydney next. Sydney was the kid no one wanted. Not because she wasn't a good athlete—she was a superb athlete, just too unruly for the Quaker student body. The accidental elbow to the face on her way down with a basketball rebound, or a pitch that narrowly missed a batter's head when the student crowded the plate, unnerved them.

She searched the benches around the circular path then moved into the grassy areas. She knew what to look for: black clothing, tiny body, long hair, fashionable expensive shoes, and a fancy handbag. She was swift but thorough. Nothing.

Jumping the fence, she headed back downtown. The intense heat of the day coupled with the half-eaten tuna sandwiches left to rot in open, overflowing garbage bins made the journey down Broadway quite malodorous. Stamped-out cigarette butts, flattened candy wrappers, and shredded newspaper littered the solar-heated concrete sidewalk as she strode past people and human silhouettes illuminated by soft streetlamp light.

She approached Union Square Park from the northwest corner. The park, founded in 1839, had a long and checkered history. In the late 1890s, it was an elegant shopping neighborhood; by the 1960s, the pop-art scene began with Andy Warhol's Factory. By the '70s, heroin addicts infiltrated the area, and it was labeled "Needle Park." The southern part of the park always served as a forum for demonstrators exercising freedom of speech. Students, runaways, and residents comingled with tourists, homeless people, and the drug-addled twenty-four hours a day.

Despite the late hour, drum circles and brass bands were banging while skateboarders and inline skaters jumped and trick rode in the moonlight. Sydney bypassed them because she knew that Lily would not be moving. She continued down to Sixteenth Street, turned left into the park, and hopped over the flimsy makeshift chain that signaled its closure for the evening. The grass was jammed with people. She asked, peered, and searched down all four aisles. It was shadowy and hard to see, so she moved up close to each bench and inspected the lifeless, spent bodies, touching nothing.

It was twelve thirty A.M. by the time she headed to Tompkins Square Park—six blocks south and four avenues east. Two nights ago she'd hit the jackpot there; she hoped to be lucky again, and she also hoped not to be.

Tompkins Square was busy but a bust. She crossed Tenth Street to a bodega to purchase a bottle of water. Two men and a woman out front were arguing about who was the best Yankees player of all time. Sydney asked her usual questions.

"I don't know nothin'," the woman said.

Sydney figured that Lily was in one of two places: holed up in a shooting gallery or a mental hospital. Or three—she could be dead. Ditto for Robbie.

Nineteen

"QUIET AROUND HERE," she said to the guard at the front of the hospital as she removed her blades.

"Yeah," he said.

"Is this typical for most days at five A.M.?"

His head cocked, and he gazed at her ID badge.

"Pretty much. Emergencies go through the ER, so all we get is husbands and some family members if someone is having a baby or dying."

"Jimmy around?"

"Mr. McClary?"

"I don't know his last name, a big guy, about two-eighty, six two, been here for years," she said.

"Yeah, Mr. McClary, except he's skinny now and he don't work the door no more. He's the night-shift supervisor now."

"I haven't seen him in ages. Is he on tonight?"

"It's Thursday. Yup, he's here. He stays in the Addison Building."

"Thanks. Maybe I'll stop by and congratulate him."

SHE CROSSED THE street, dashing into a twenty-four-hour deli. She picked up some apples, two bananas, a few waters, coffee, and donuts. Several doors down sat the Addison Building, an annexed building that kept the hospital running. It housed the mechanicals and the security systems. Sydney's hands were full as she knocked on the front door with her right foot. A tall, broad man with thinning red hair and a frown opened it. At the sight of Sydney, his ruddy face lit into a bright smile, exposing crooked yellow teeth.

"Well, well! Been a long time. And what are you doing here at this hour?" he said, reaching for the bundles.

"Hey, Jimmy. I need to ask your opinion about something. I brought you some coffee and stuff."

He peeked into the bags. "Aren't you sweet, Doctor. I'm gonna have to pass on the donuts, though. Don't want to ruin my new gorgeous figure," he said, caressing his hip with his free hand.

"You look fantastic. And what happened to the uniform?"

"I got promoted, Doc. I'm the night supervisor. Gotta look the part, my dear." He chuckled. She smiled. "Sit, sit," he said.

She explained her relationship with Robbie, then paused. "Do they have any other leads from inside the hospital? Or is it just the blond woman and boy?"

"As far as I know, they're not gonna look inside the hospital anymore. They turned the place inside out, vetted the patients and staff, came up with nothing. The hospital brass is very happy about that." He reached for a red apple, wiped it on has pant leg, examined it, and took a huge bite.

"So how do they explain what the blonde and the boy were doing at the hospital?" She looked straight at him.

"I don't know. They don't share all of their information with us. Unfortunately, the hospital's a big place with lots of strangers coming in day and night. We get all kinds of people. Some even hide out and live here for months. One homeless man lived in one of the offices for over a month; he overslept and was found by the cleaning staff. We had another one who lived in a call room for about three months. And then we had a woman living in the risk management offices when they were under construction for five months! The morning crews found her. Doc, this kidnapping is not a hospital problem. It was outside of the hospital, and, like I said, the administration is thrilled about that." He shook his head in sympathy and peered into her squinted eyes. "I wish I had better news. All I can say is stay out of it. Let the professionals do their job."

With half-closed eyes, she took a deep, measured breath and practiced a walking meditation across the street and into the quiet hallways of the hospital.

Why would the authorities give up on the hospital before they find out who that blonde is, and what she was doing here? If the woman is a simple indigent like Jimmy implied, she's pretty damn good at eluding the authorities. And what about the car that picked her up? Do they think Hasina's involved? She was the only one who knew that Robbie would be there that day. Crap, forty-eight hours is up. They're failing.

Sydney unlocked her hospital mailbox. Inside there were three sealed white envelopes, folded and flattened to fit through the box's slit. All three had her name scribbled on the front; all three had different penmanship.

Twenty

THE FIRST NOTE read:

> Used condoms found on twenty-third floor.

The second read:

> Homeless man from the ER wandered into the hospital same day, same time the boy went missing.

The third envelope held a personnel list from Smikes.

Disturbed but encouraged that the staff was on the lookout, she decided to pursue the second lead on her first break. She grabbed some scrubs; the phone rang.

"Syd. I'm in Downtown Hospital. Lily OD'd," her mother said. Sydney's heartbeat pounded in her ears.

"Is she alive?"

"She's being revived. Can you come here?"

"They scheduled me back-to-back today. It'll screw up the whole OR schedule." Sydney paused and sucked on her lower lip. "Look, there's nothing I can do anyway. Let the doctors handle it. Are you alone?"

"David's here."

"Good. She's lucky her boyfriend shows up for her."

"I guess."

"Is she coherent?" Sydney asked.

"Not so much."

"Do they expect her to live, Ma?"

"I think so. No one told me to brace myself."

"You all right?"

"Yeah, yeah. It's the same thing over and over again. How many times is Lily going do this?"

"Ma, it's not about the drugs. She has a borderline personality. She doesn't do this on purpose."

"She has terrible idiosyncrasies. She needs to grow up."

"She needs more help."

"All we do is give her help. She's been in every psych program and rehab program in the city."

"How did she get to the hospital?"

"David carried her in."

"Do you think she'll be released today?"

"Who knows?"

"Well, at least we know where she is now. And at least she's being attended to," Sydney said in a soft voice. "I'll be there by six, at the latest. If she's released before then, beep me."

Sydney touched her red-hot cheek. She dropped her forehead on the desk and closed her eyes. She heard a quiet noise—it sounded like a small animal scratching on her door. She focused and listened to the faint scratch and knock—it sounded like someone was using their nails instead of their knuckles.

"Yes," she called out.

"Dr. Chang, it's Grace," said the hushed voice. "I saw the light under your door."

"Grace?" she said as she hopped up in socks and opened it. Grace greeted her with a solemn expression.

"Come in. Is something wrong?"

Grace's forehead pointed down at her white, polished work shoes. Her eyes slowly rose and met Sydney's. Grace had cleaned the hospital for the past twenty years and worked on Sydney's floor for the past eight. She was a quiet woman in her midforties who'd met her husband, Isaiah Jordan, over a plate of roast beef in the cafeteria fifteen years earlier. They lived in Brooklyn with three-year-old twin boys whom Sydney met at birth, when Sydney did Grace's epidural. With silky brown skin, full lips, and round eyes, Grace possessed a warm and lovely smile in a sparrowlike body frame. She was a serious woman who exuded a gentle kindness, and Sydney liked her.

"Well, Dr. Chang, I, I don't know. But, I, well, I thought I'd tell you about something—well, I'm not sure." Grace focused on her feet. Her left middle finger fiddled with her hairnet.

"Grace, it's okay. Is it about work? And by the way, I thought we were over the *doctor* stuff. Or should I call you *Mrs. Jordan*?"

"Okay, Sydney. Okay." She smiled shyly. Then she pointed to Robbie's photo. Sydney raised her index finger to her mouth, shook her head, and led Grace out of the office. The hallway was empty. They walked down the entire length of the corridor and turned right. Sydney pointed. Grace reached for her keys, put them in the lock, and they entered the utility closet. Sydney moved to the sink, turning the water on full force.

She whispered close to Grace's ear, "If it's about Robbie, let's speak in private."

"I just thought I should show you something. Isaiah and I spoke about it, and seeing how worried you are, and, you know, I've been dusting his pictures in your office for a couple of years now, you know, and, well, I got to thinking…"

"Show me what?" Sydney said quietly staring into Grace's blinking eyes.

"I just can't lose my job, you know. Isaiah said you came down to the sub and you was really worried...." Grace met Sydney's stare with a pained, tortured expression.

"I understand, Grace. I know how hard this is for you. What did you want to show me?"

Grace reached into the pocket of her blue hospital uniform, pulling out a brown paper bag. She extended her arm. With care, Sydney peeled back the fold and pulled out a small-sized plastic bag. She looked through it, then reached into a bin of purple nitrile gloves. Gloved, she unzipped the plastic bag and removed a smaller baggie. Inside it was a blood-tinged condom.

"Where did you find this, Grace?" she asked.

"In a garbage can outside a doctor's office, where the secretaries are at." Grace looked up at the ceiling.

"When?"

"The morning Robbie went missing." Sydney stiffened. Her heart pounded. Her breath thickened.

"Was it just lying in the garbage can? Can you tell me which doctor's office this was?"

"Um-hmm. There were a few wet paper towels mixed in and when I dumped the can into my main garbage container, I saw it go over. It stuck out because it had blood on it. I never see no bloody garbage in the doctors' offices, you know, or in the secretary pools. When I worked in the OR or in the patient exam rooms, sure, but nowhere else. I never see nothing bloody in the doctors' offices. Well, almost never."

"You've found something like this before?" Sydney controlled her breathing.

"Yes."

"In the same area, near the same doctor's office?"

"Yes, what's odd is that these were bloody. I mean, we've all found condoms here and there, but none of them was bloody. I found condoms twice before in a doctor's office area a few years back and on the twenty-fifth-floor stairwell. But those weren't bloody."

"When was the last time you found a bloody condom in this doctor's office?"

"About three months ago. They stood out. The red color, you know, mixed in with all that white paper. Plus, they supposed to put bloody things in the hazard garbage cans."

"Why did you decide to take it this time, Grace?"

"Well, I was upset the other times too, but I figured it was none my business, you know? Isaiah told me to just stay out of it. Mind my own beeswax. So I did. This time, well, I don't know why, I just saved it. I hid it someplace good, and I was gonna throw it out cuz what would I really be able to do, but then the boy went missing. I thought about giving it to the police, but when I heard you'd been downstairs looking... Then yesterday, when you gave us that talk about finding any little thing, well, I decided I should bring it to you."

"I know it wasn't easy. Thank you, Grace. I need to know which office area you found this in."

Grace adjusted her hairnet, rubbing her nose with the back of her hand.

"I'll do my best to keep you out of this. I really appreciate it." Sydney's left eye twitched.

"It's just that, well, he's a powerful doctor." Fear ripped across Grace's eyes. "It was outside of Dr. Inger's office."

"Bob Inger?" Sydney asked, trying to control her shock. *Shit. Two days ago he helped out during the CODE. He's one of the few I actually respect as a doctor. But all of the doors open with a master key. Who has them? Who gets them? Housekeeping, engineering, security? Maybe someone just dropped it in there?*

Sydney closed her eyes. "Dr. Inger is one of the most respected and powerful doctors here," she said. "Everyone likes him."

"Not everyone."

"Grace, did you find anything else that seemed suspicious?"

"Just a lot of wet paper towels and some bloody and slimy tissues. It was nasty. Oh yeah, and a used tube of that KY jelly. The stuff they have in the OB area."

Sydney swallowed. "And exactly what time did you find all of this, Grace?"

"Right after I started my shift, so seven fifteen. I clean his room first. When I came out to dump out the cans in the outer office, I found it."

"Was there anything odd in his actual office?"

"Not that I noticed."

"Was everything wet when you found it? "

"Yes, looked like everything was just used."

Sydney's beeper zinged. She was wanted in the OR.

"I really appreciate you coming forward like this, Grace. It probably has nothing to do with Robbie. The timing is off. There's no way Robbie could have walked through the halls and downstairs without being visibly upset at six forty-five or seven."

"Can't be good. There's somethin' 'bout that man."

"I need you to hang on to this for now. Let me think about it. Put it someplace safe, but someplace you can get to easily. And one more thing—have you heard about the homeless man who was wandering the halls the morning Robbie went missing?"

"Oh, they found that guy passed out in a bathroom."

"Does the staff know that they found him?"

"Guess some folks do and some folks don't."

Twenty-One

SYDNEY WAS ROUNDING the corner about to enter OR 2 when Dr. Inger hurried past, smiled, waved, and continued to OR 3. She forced herself to raise a hand in greeting.

Throughout the day she monitored heart rates, blood pressures, respiratory rates, and consciousness. She controlled, calibrated, and adjusted meds. Sydney was in her zone, a brief return to normalcy.

When the last case finished, she found the closest stairwell and took the steps by two, charging down five flights. *Hopefully, Lily won't have any long-term damage from this. Hopefully, she won't have seizures like she did after the last OD. Hopefully, Robbie's not being tortured.* She arrived in front of a lab with a wide window. Larry Weinstein, a brilliant diminutive scientist, was sitting behind a black lab table, alone. He and Sydney had known each other for years, since medical school.

"Hey Larry. I have a question for you. Maybe you can help me figure something out."

"I doubt it, but I'll give it my best shot for you, Sydney." Rubbing his trim beard with his thumb and index finger, he smiled shyly.

"I went over some amniotic fluid embolism research this morning and wondered, does adult DNA differ from children's? Just based on the age. Would it differ?"

"Yes, telomere length decreases with age. There's been a lot of work done, but the results often vary by technique and lab. But telomere length does decrease with age. If I recall, a lab in Japan did research on this and found fairly consistent results with only a small variability, but perhaps that was because they used a homogeneous Japanese population. The thing is, Sydney, it's hard to measure because everyone's telomeres start out at different lengths. How short they become is based on where they begin. Let's just say there's tremendous individual variation. Want me to look up the Japanese lab for you as a starting point?"

"No thanks...It should be easy enough for me to find. I need to ask them some questions. Do you mind if I use your name to break the ice?"

"Sydney, you know I would love to give you my name, especially my last name." He beamed and adjusted the suspenders that held up his faded, baggy jeans.

"Thanks, funny man."

Heading back upstairs, she churned. *It's not Robbie's DNA. Time frame's wrong. But if the DNA from the blood on the condom is from a child, I have a place to start. A gross place, but a place.*

Twenty-Two

It was five o'clock. She hadn't heard from her mother. Lily could have severe brain damage, and her mother might not call. At Eighty-Sixth Street and Lexington Avenue, she hopped on the downtown number four express train to Fourteenth Street.

The bleak and shabby Downtown Hospital ER entrance led into a winding, dark hallway with light tan walls and chipped, yellow-and-green tiled floors. Bluish-white fluorescent lights cast a gray, purplish haze. At the end of the dreary corridor sat a glass-enclosed intake office that seemed like it had been airlifted out of a high-security prison and dropped intact, bars and all. To the left was a small, grimy ER waiting area. It looked like it reeked, but oddly, it didn't. Even a fresh coat of paint would spruce it up. It hadn't been exactly glamorous the last time Lily overdosed three years ago, but it hadn't looked like this either.

Rows of cold metal chairs and hard benches were screwed into the floor of the waiting room. A twenty-four-inch TV hung from the ceiling playing *Law & Order*.

Her mother and David were in the rear of the room with their spines pressed against the backs of the hard chairs, necks craned, and eyes transfixed on the television. They didn't notice her arrival. Sydney thought her mother looked frail and ghastly gray, even though she was as elegant as always, in navy linen slacks and a crisp white linen blouse. David was his usual self: greasy shoulder-length brown hair in a ponytail, ripped oversized jeans, and a tattered, formerly white T-shirt. A thin veil of sweat covered his face and neck. His right hand had a tremor, which signaled to Sydney that he was in need of a fix.

David was about six feet tall with broad shoulders, hazel eyes, and a strong New York Italian accent. He and Lily dated on and off for close to a decade. Hooked on heroin for over fourteen years, David moved around a lot. He lived on the street, in shelters, and at home with his mother until she kicked him out. For a brief stint, he lived with Lily when she had her own apartment in Flushing, Queens. He worked part-time as a taxi driver on Long Island these days and rented a room in a house in Mineola. High, strung out, or straight, he looked out for his tiny-boned Lily, and when things went wrong on the street, he always took the hit for her. He'd been beaten, threatened, and had even spent a few nights in jail in her place. Sydney and her mother thought he was a good guy, but drug-free, he'd be even better.

Sydney ambled over and sat down. They glanced at her, nodded with glassy eyes, then turned back to the television screen. They had been there since six A.M., and Sydney recognized their hospital fugue state.

"Can anyone update me?" Sydney asked.

"One minute; we're at the good part," her mother said and continued to stare at the television.

"Am I correct in assuming that Lily's doing reasonably well?"

"We spoke to her. She said it was an accident," David said as he, too, stared at the show.

"Where did you find her?" Sydney said.

"A guy I know called me to come get her," David said.

"They gave her a drug to reverse the drug she took, and they're monitoring her. When I asked about ten minutes ago, they said they wanted to watch her a little longer and if she was fine, they'd release her, and we could take her home," her mother said.

"So they're not going to keep her for twenty-four hours. Is she mentally with it?"

"As mentally with it as she always is. You know your sister."

"Ma, you look like you need something to drink and eat."

"Well, I feel horrible."

"I'll get you something. David, you want anything?"

"I'll go with you and help you carry the stuff, Syd."

"Great. Ma, I know what you like. I'll find something."

"Yes, and a martini would be nice too."

"Funny," Sydney said.

"I'm not being funny. I need a drink."

Sydney and David walked into the steamy evening.

They continued in silence for a block when David turned to Sydney. "Not for nothin', Syd, but I think you should know somethin'," he said as he hobbled from a broken ankle that hadn't healed correctly.

"What's that?"

"Well, about two weeks ago, maybe three, when Lily was at the morgue—you know, her funeral program thing?"

"Yeah."

"Well, she called me all freaked out. She was cryin' and so upset. Syd, I never heard her like that before. I was worried, you know?"

"What was it?"

"A girl named Maddy, or something—no, not Maddy, like Mona, uh, Marsha, an old friend of Lily's, someone she was best friends with for a long time back in high school."

"Marcy?"

"Yeah, yeah, Marcy. Well, she came in dead and Lily had to prepare her body, do her makeup and stuff, and it completely wigged her out. You know?"

"Marcy was Lily's best friend from third grade until they graduated. They were inseparable; they also started drugs together," Sydney said.

"How long did they stay friends for?" he asked.

"Well, they went to different colleges, and as far as I know, they lost touch about nine or ten years ago."

"Yeah, cuz I never heard nothin' about no Marcy until the other night."

"Did Lily mention how she died?"

"She was drugged out. Walked into the street in the middle of the night, someplace dark with real bad lighting, and got hit by a car. Some place uptown—like real uptown."

"You said this happened about three weeks ago?"

"Yeah, yeah, Syd. It really whacked her out."

"It makes sense now. Thanks for saving her again, David."

"You don't need to thank me, Syd. I love your sister."

Sydney looked at David and smiled. He looked back, then turned away and looked at the pavement. They continued in silence.

In the corner deli, Sydney bought a turkey sandwich and a bottle of water for her mother; a Nestlé Crunch bar, Little Debbie cupcakes, and a Coke for David; and a salami-and-American cheese hero with extra mayo and a Coke for herself. As she paid, David grabbed all the bags from her. When Sydney went to help him, he refused.

"Come on, Syd, what kind of a gentleman would I be if I let you carry the bags? Come on," he said.

Just as they finished their dinner, they were summoned "to the back." Rows of beds were lined up; blue sheets hung from curtain rods surrounding each bed, serving as makeshift walls. Groans, sighs, and shouts of pain echoed throughout the crowded space.

Lily's ribs jutted out as she stood hunched over a narrow bed with the back of her hospital gown wide open. She finished signing her release papers and handed them over to the nurse as they entered. Her mother and David sauntered toward her. Sydney hung back.

Lily's once-silky hair hung limp and lifeless down her cheeks. Her coloring, usually the hue of a warm biscuit, was icy blue. The nurse gave their mother a bag of Lily's clothing and she passed them to Lily. They stank.

"Throw those in the garbage, Ma. I stopped by your house and brought some clean clothes. Here," Sydney said as she reached over and handed them to Lily.

"No. Don't throw my clothes out. I like that shirt, and the skirt is Armani. Put it back in the bag; we'll take it home," Lily said in an agitated, raspy voice.

"You okay, Lily?" Sydney asked.

"Good, good. I'm good," Lily said as she avoided eye contact and bounced her head like a little plastic puppy on the dashboard of a car.

"Let's go already," their mother said in a booming voice. "Been stuck here all day. I'm tired of this."

"Let Lily put her clothes on, Ma. We'll wait outside."

Curved over, Lily reached up and pulled the blue curtain around the bed.

Minutes later, in a floral blouse, denim shorts, and purple flip-flops, Lily shuffled out. She hung behind them as they walked the five blocks in silence to Twenty-First Street. When they approached the front of the building, David nodded and raised his hand.

"Lil. See you later, babe."

As soon as their mother opened the door to the apartment, Lily blurted, "I'm going to sleep," and started for her room. Sydney's eyes moved to her sister. Hunched over, smelling like old vomit with skin both translucent and pasty, Lily made her way down the long hallway; Sydney's lips twisted to the side as her eyes followed.

"Lily, David told me about Marcy," she called out after her.

Just as she was about to make a left into her room, Lily stopped. Her head jutted up, and she turned and looked right at Sydney for the first time that day. "Yeah."

"You want to tell me about it," Sydney asked.

"Nothing to tell."

"It's upsetting," Sydney said.

"Uh-huh."

Twenty-Three

SYDNEY IGNORED THE flashing voice-mail light in her bedroom, rethought it, and pressed play. There were two new messages from Mick. She grabbed her laptop and a canteen of water and headed out. Shrugging, she stopped, turned around, picked up the phone, and punched in a number.

It kicked her to voice mail. "Mick. Sydney. Sorry I haven't been in touch. I'm in the middle of two things right now, and I don't have a minute. I'll call you as soon as these situations are handled."

At the electronics store across the street, she paid cash for a private web browser USB plug-in. In Madison Square Park, a free Wi-Fi zone, she slipped the anonymous proxy server router into her laptop. She knew that nothing was completely anonymous, but this would make it harder to track. She had no reason to believe she was being watched, and no reason to believe she wasn't.

At close to eight thirty P.M., the park looked like Macy's a day before Christmas. The food emporium, Eataly, directly across the street plus the myriad of food trucks kept the area packed with hungry tourists and locals. Sydney found an unoccupied patch of grass on the eastern edge and settled in around folks eating food from Shake Shack.

Using the anonymous search engine DuckDuckGo, she typed: "DNA," "DNA AND Telomeres," and finally "DNA fingerprinting." She cross-referenced "DNA AND telomeres AND age." The study Larry referenced popped up on ScienceDirect in the periodical called *Forensic Science International*, and it included the scientists' names and their university affiliation.

Larry was correct. Telomeres, the base pair sequences at the ends of each chromosome that act like plastic caps at the tips of shoelaces, shortened with age. There was also a lot of length variability based on the type of test used. The lab in Japan had tested dried blood using the Southern blot analysis and reported the least variability. They were able to determine the age of their subjects within a four-year span. Other labs using the qPCR (quantitative polymerase chain reaction) test had a larger variability of plus or minus thirteen years. The authorities don't use telomere testing because legally the tests are too variable to make a case.

She continued to research the kind of specimens suitable for this DNA analysis and the preparation, dry or wet. She confirmed that sperm only appeared in postpubertal males. After gathering all of the needed information, she studied miscarriage, chromosomal abnormalities, and in vitro fertilization—just in case she was being monitored.

If the blood belongs to a child, the sperm DNA needs to be matched to an individual. The blood won't be Robbie's. Should I give the condom to the authorities, then? They'll have an easier time matching the sperm and blood DNA to an individual if they can get everyone in the hospital to submit to testing. Big "if." Even if they match the sperm, without the proper chain of evidence, the court case is unwinnable. Everyone there has access to blood. So the condom won't help them. It'll involve Grace and probably rattle any kidnapping connection into cutting their losses. I'll do it myself.

Twenty-four

PROPPING HER DOOR open, Sydney padded to the end of her apartment hallway and slipped a folded note under her neighbor's door.

> Atsuko,
> I'd like to speak to you later if you are around. I'll knock on your door at eleven P.M.
> Thanks,
> *Sydney*

Atsuko and Sydney were neighbors for around three years. Both women were reserved, both exceptionally polite. They'd dined together a few times but knew very little about each other. Still, they shared a strong unspoken connection.

At eleven, Sydney knocked softly on Atsuko's door. Atsuko answered in a short black kimono detailed with white and pale pink orchids. In her late thirties, unmarried, with no children and no clear work schedule, Atsuko was, as always, elegant. Above average in height with long wavy auburn hair, she traveled often and dressed exclusively in French designer clothing accessorized by exquisite jewels. Nothing much seemed to worry Atsuko.

"Sydney, good evening. Everything okay?" she asked in a delicate voice.

"Okay," Sydney replied with a smile then a grimace. "I need to ask you a big favor."

"Come in. Come in," she said, gently touching Sydney's arm.

"I appreciate this," Sydney said.

"No problem at all. Would you like tea?"

"No, thank you."

They faced each other on an overstuffed white L-shaped sofa covered with diminutive cream-colored silk pillows. Two small lamps cast a soft orange glow, illuminating maple hardwood floors, antique Asian furniture, and shimmering silver-gold walls.

"Will you call a lab in Japan and ask them if we can pay them to process a DNA specimen? I'd call, but I don't want my name used in association with it."

"Why not?" Atsuko asked.

"It's complicated. I can't say," Sydney said, then paused. "Should I leave so you can think it over?"

"Is this very important to you, Sydney?"

"Very."

"What do you need me to ask?" Atsuko moved to her desk and took out a sheet of paper.

"Please tell them that an independent researcher has read their telomere data. He wants to send a dry blood specimen that may be mixed with other types of cells from two people to determine the approximate age of each individual. Please ask if they'll consider doing this. Please tell them that the researcher will be happy to pay for all of their time and expenses."

Atsuko placed her hand on top of the phone on the elaborately carved dark cherrywood desk. Sydney offered a calling card. Atsuko shook her head no and plugged in the number Sydney read out to her.

After speaking for a few minutes, Atsuko placed her hand over the phone's mouthpiece. "Scientist say this lab is done with that project. They are on new one."

Sydney had been afraid of that. "Please tell him that the researcher values their professional opinion and before committing to a larger trial wants more detailed information. Since the original groundbreaking work emanated from their lab on a homogeneous population using only blood samples, he wants to send them a mixed specimen on a heterogeneous population. He wants to know if it's even possible to analyze a specimen of this kind." Atsuko scribbled it down.

"He say they are not a pay lab. He say this was research project and not taking random specimens for money. They have published paper and moved on. Thank you very much but not interested."

Sydney blanched.

Atsuko hung up and sat by Sydney's side. "Please tell me why you need this."

Sydney shook her head. "Can you think of anything that can be said to convince them, Atsuko?"

Atsuko looked down at her creamy, folded hands resting in her lap. Then she stood, walked back to the desk, picked up the phone, and redialed. She spoke quickly and quietly. After a few minutes, she said, *"Arigatou gozaimasu."*

When Atsuko faced Sydney again, she was as elegant and as delicate as ever; however, there was a subtle change. Her facial skin had darkened slightly and a sheer veil of hardness had lowered onto her soft brown eyes. She spoke slowly. "The lab will fax me on how they want specimen sent. I will rewrite in English and slip under your door tonight."

"What just happened?" Sydney asked with her mouth ajar.

"No need worry, Sydney. When you have specimen ready tomorrow, bring to me, and I will ship to Japan overnight.

They promise to fax me results in four, five days of receiving specimen."

"You're incredible, Atsuko. I...I don't know what to say."

"My pleasure, Sydney." Atsuko nodded. "I hope this helps your problem."

AT FIVE THIRTY the next morning, Friday, Sydney was showered and dressed. There was no note under her door. *Did the lab change their mind? Did Atsuko fall asleep?* She slipped on her socks and was about to leave when the phone rang.

"Baby, it's Mick. Sorry to call so early, but I can never reach you. Everything okay?"

"Things have been insane. Family stuff. Work."

"Oh, okay. Just wanted to make sure you were okay, and that, you know, we're okay," he said.

Sydney thought. *We?* "Everything's fine. I'll call you when things calm down."

"When do you think that'll be, babe?"

"Can't say. I have to run to work. I'll call you soon. Have a good day."

Walking to her front door, she slipped. A beautiful piece of fine vintage stationery flew out from under her foot.

Twenty-five

PLANTED IN FRONT of the hospital's staff parking garage, between First and East End Avenues, Sydney waited. A lime-green baseball cap topped her head and streamline steel-rimmed blackout sunglasses covered her eyes. Lifting her cap, she wiped the moisture from her forehead with the back of her hand. She surveyed the street, still quiet and soupy hot. Her pants and shirt were soaked through, the back of her neck was sticky with salt, and she longed for a shower. She doused her head with water from her metal bottle and relished in its coolness as it poured down her neck and flowed onto her back. This tiny street shower would have to suffice.

Few cars passed, as it was only 6:20 A.M. A white smudged New York sanitation truck picked up a heap of odiferous trash from the corner. She was relieved when the garbage was taken but underwhelmed by the stench that lingered. A lone yellow cab inched by on the lookout for a fare while delivery trucks squeaked to a stop dropping off food at the corner delis. It was her favorite time of day.

She held a coffee in one hand and a P. D. James novel in the other. Her love for a good mystery had started as a young girl and hadn't abated. Every few minutes she glanced up to check the ebb and flow of traffic—she wanted to know exactly what time the street turned from languid to energetic. She reached into the deli bag and pulled out a jelly donut wrapped in plastic. Tearing the wrapping, she bit into it without much hope since it wasn't freshly made, but when a sizable plop of strawberry gel oozed out, she was pleasantly surprised.

The action picked up at 6:47. Once her colleagues began pulling into the garage, she kept the book in her hand but stopped reading. Her eyes peered over the paperback and focused on each car that entered and exited. It was expensive to park in Manhattan, even with the hospital's insider price. Most people took the train or bus to work; a few lucky ones got dropped off by friends and family.

Her mind stewed. *Robbie had to be driven away. But there are people around. How did they get the kid into their car without him making a fuss? How were the blond woman and child involved other than sharing a few words with him? And the condom in Inger's front office, is it relevant? Is Inger connected in any way? Lots of people have access to that office.*

As the nurses left the garage and spotted Sydney on the curb, those who knew her broke into bemused expressions; those who knew her better just smiled and said good morning. Most of the doctors didn't even notice her.

Minutes passed, and the sun's rays grew hotter. Sydney became stickier and stiller as she sat on the curb reading.

At 6:55, the one she'd been waiting for rolled in; a dark green, shiny new BMW 725i sedan with vanity plates: RSI. A few minutes later a man in his early fifties, about six feet tall, with perfect posture, a thick mane of brushed-back silver-streaked hair, and a beautiful, even tan sauntered out. Dr. Bob Inger smiled widely and looked down. "Good morning, Sydney. What are you doing on the curb?" he asked.

"Relaxing," she answered, looking up.

"On the curb? Surely there are nicer spots," he chuckled. "By the way, I meant to call you. Remember the VIP I mentioned a few days ago? Well, he's scheduled for today. I signed you up for it. I hope that's okay."

"No problem."

"Enjoy the curb."

Now Robbie's been gone for over seventy-two hours. Her half-wave was accompanied by a side smile.

Twenty-Six

SYDNEY HALF JOGGED through the empty hallways—no Grace. Checking one last side corridor, she spotted the back of a cleaning cart jutting out of an office.

Sydney poked her head into the empty, stale-smelling office and called out, "Grace?"

"Yes," Grace responded from around the bend.

Sydney entered and smiled.

Her eyes darted around Sydney's face.

Sydney whispered into her ear, "I need the bag. Let's meet in the same place as last time. Charles—uh, Dr. Lansing is in the office." Grace rolled the cart into the room and locked the door.

Grace was lingering outside the cleaning utility room when Sydney approached in fresh scrubs. She pushed her key into the door lock. Inside, she handed Sydney the brown bag.

"Hang on a minute," Sydney whispered. Gloved, she pulled a sterile pack and five two-by-three-inch glassine envelopes out of her scrub pocket. "Grace, please put gloves on so you can hold these for me."

Sydney handed her the envelopes and then opened the sterile kit carefully, placing it on the flat surface of the sink counter. She extricated the condom from the bag. Grace flinched.

Holding the condom, Sydney used a sterile scissor, made four long slices down the tip, then severed each slice with a horizontal cut about one and one-half inches from the tip. She dropped each section into a separate envelope that Grace held open. Grace bit her lower lip.

"Thank you. I know it's not pleasant. I really appreciate your help."

"Had to, for the boy and for you."

"Why don't you leave first? I'll wait a few minutes," Sydney said.

Grace turned to leave, then pivoted back. With tear-filled eyes, she stepped forward and extended an awkward side hug. Sydney stiffened, then smiled.

Sydney threw the lock in an individual bathroom, then flushed the condom and tossed the brown bag into the trash.

Alone in her office with fresh gloves on, she slipped two envelopes into a five-by-eight-inch manila envelope, taped it closed, and placed it in her backpack hanging in the closet behind her desk. The other three, she dropped into a plain white letter-sized envelope and tossed it in a lower desk drawer.

She picked up the phone and dialed. "Ma, how's Lily?"

"I wouldn't know."

"Did she leave the apartment?"

"No, she's still in her room, I guess."

"Well, did you check on her this morning?"

"No."

"Do me a favor, go in and see if she's breathing."

"Hold on."

Her mother's light blue velvet slippers clopped away on the dark-stained oak floor. Silence. A few minutes, the click-clops grew closer and louder.

"She looks fine," she said, "but I don't know anything about breathing."

Twenty-Seven

SYDNEY KNOCKED HARD on the door to Dr. Inger's outer office suite.

"I wanted to see if you needed anything special for the setup today," she said.

"How thoughtful. How about a coffee?"

"I don't have time for coffee."

Following a straight-backed Inger through the secretarial area and into his personal office, she surreptitiously eyed all of the doors' locking mechanisms. His cologne permeated the air as she memorized details about the physical layout of both rooms.

An oversized window sat behind his desk. It was only a few feet from the building across the way, and with the shades up, as he had them now, you could see right in. *Backlighting will be a problem here.*

"Anything unusual I need to know about your patient? Heart disease, any lung or kidney trouble? Do you want anything in particular from me?" she asked.

"Not that I can think of. Graham Stone is an old friend and one of our board members. He's one of the leading businessmen in the country. We golf together."

Sydney glanced at the angles of the room in relation to where the door opened. She noted where the desk and couch were located and glimpsed at the desktop. There was only one photo; it was of a regal-looking, middle-aged blond woman and two teenage girls. Off to the side were five Matchbox racing cars—an orange Porsche, old light blue Ford Mustang, bright red MBX Coupe, white Stingray convertible, and a silver Aston Martin. Sydney knew these cars well; she'd played with them nonstop when she was little.

"Is that right?" she said. *Until I lower those blinds, I'll have to work in complete darkness.*

"Yes, he started Stone Industries."

"Can't say that I'm familiar with it. But if he's in good health, I'll see you in the OR."

The thyroidectomy took place in an OR off of a sparkling corridor with floor-to-ceiling windows overlooking the East River. Each time the doors opened, the fluorescent illumination comingled with streams of sunlight and bounced up and around the gray-speckled linoleum floor.

Greetings were exchanged, requests for equipment discussed, and baseball highlights debated. The cacophony of the OR theater was similar to the buzz in the wings of a Broadway show minutes before the curtain rises.

There were two nurses this morning: one circulating and one scrubbed. One selected the equipment—scalpels, sutures, lap pads, clamps—and anything else that Inger required. The other manned a mobile stainless steel table covered in a sterile drape and filled with equipment that's handed to the surgeon as needed. Both nurses counted the supplies and equipment before the operation started and again right before the patient's surgical incision was closed, making sure that nothing was inadvertently left inside.

The patient, Graham Stone, lumbered over to the six-foot-long, two-and-one-half-foot-wide metal bed. Electric and movable, the bed was covered with black plastic foam sectionals that shifted in tandem with the metal sections. He lay down. Sydney took a quick look at her notes and then at her patient: white, pasty gray, fifty-five years old, five foot eight, 205 pounds, brownish-gray crew cut. She greeted him, introduced herself, asked her usual questions, and asked him if he had any. He didn't.

The door to the OR whisked open, and Dr. Inger entered; bright sunlight backlit his body. With his face mask on, his twinkling eyes were smiling.

Stone lifted his head and turned toward him.

"How are ya, big guy?" Inger asked. "Are you going to the fund-raiser next week?"

"I plan on it if you don't kill me today."

They chuckled. Sydney grimaced behind her face mask.

"Let me do my thing. Next week we'll have a toast together, Graham."

"I'm giving you medicine through your IV now. Have pleasant dreams," Sydney said.

The patient closed his eyes. Within seconds he was asleep. A breathing tube was placed, and he was prepped and covered with sterile drapes.

The overhead operating lights flipped on. Inger left to scrub, and when he returned, he took center stage. Scalpel in hand, he made a precise incision into the patient's neck.

The circulating nurse looked at Sydney. "I know you're close to Dr. Wagner, Dr. Chang. Any word on her missing child?" she asked.

"Not that I know of."

"Heartbreaking," the nurse replied and sniffed.

"Horrible," Inger said as he inserted an instrument deep into Stone's neck. After a brief pause, Inger looked up at Sydney.

Sydney kept her head down and her eyes on the patient.

"Other than the very upsetting news, is anything new or interesting going on?" he asked as he slid retractors into the incision.

"Nope. How about you?"

"Well, my eldest daughter was made a goalie on her soccer team this season. That's the big news in our house," he said.

"Uh-huh," she replied. She stared at the monitors. Inger continued to cut and explore. He worked at a rapid pace with tremendous exactitude. *He really is a talented surgeon.*

"Did you get a chance to vacation this summer?" Inger asked.

"Not yet. How about you?"

"Well, I'm taking Monday off because it's my twentieth wedding anniversary, and then I'm taking my family to Italy in two weeks."

In two weeks! "Happy anniversary. How long are you going for?"

"Three weeks."

Two and one-half hours later, as the operation was finishing, Sydney asked, "On call tonight, Bob?"

"Technically, no, but I'll be working late. It may be so late that I'll be too exhausted to drive home."

"You sleep here even when you're not on call?" Sydney asked.

"I do. I draw the line at one A.M. If a case ends after that and I'm working the next day, I stay. If not, I take a nap then leave."

"Yeah. Like most of us."

Walking out of the OR, as usual, Inger removed his face mask, put his chewed gum in it, and threw the combination into the garbage can by the scrub sink. Knowing his routine, Sydney followed him to the door. After he rounded the corner, with a freshly gloved hand, she bent down and pretended to throw her mask away. She picked up Inger's discarded mask, placing it in a clean glove. She pushed it deep into her scrub pants pocket.

Twenty-Eight

SMIKES WAS IN the subbasement, head down, clipboard in hand, rushing down a stuffy hallway.

"Hey, Smikes!" He stopped and looked up.

"Sydney." He placed his clipboard under his right armpit, clapped his hands together, and frowned. "I don't have any new updates from down here. I'm sorry."

"Don't be. Nothing upstairs, either. But I do need to find a ladder." His eyebrows furrowed. "I want to hang some things."

He cocked his head. She smiled. Smikes rolled his eyes. "Wait here. I may have one hanging around." A few minutes later, he returned with a medium-sized ladder.

"One more thing, Smikes. Since I'll be hanging a bunch of pictures and stuff, I was wondering if you could tell me if anyone, like painters or electricians, will be anywhere in my building tonight or Monday night in case I hit a beam or something and need help. You know, just in case."

"Hit a beam or something?"

"I won't, but it would be good to know if someone's around to help in case something unexpected happens."

"You're something, Doc. Let me see here." He flipped through his clipboard and found the appropriate one. "Well, you're out of luck. Your building doesn't have any work scheduled until next month. But if you're really in a bind, it looks like the Carson Building, fifth, sixth, and seventh floors, has a bunch of construction jobs going on right now. So walk over there and see if you can snag someone to help you if you need it. Hopefully, you won't need it."

"Great, thanks. And thanks so much for that scheduling paper."

"I looked," Smikes said. "Randall was assigned to that floor that night. Been here for years, Sydney. One of my best."

IT WAS LATE afternoon when her cases finished, and she ran by the fourth floor. The makeshift FBI office was gone and so were the agents.

Across the street, she entered a small redbrick building.

"Luther!" she bellowed. The grind and swoosh of the washing machines and dryers filled with greens and grays made hearing a Herculean task.

"Dr. Chang! Well, well, long time no see," said a slightly hunched-over six-footer with long gray braids and a toothy smile.

"How are you, your grandkids?"

"Can't complain, can't complain. Next month I'll have forty-five years on the job—ain't that something?"

"Wow. I didn't realize that it's been that long. I bet you're looking to retire soon."

"Not a chance. I can't stay home with the wife all day."

They laughed.

"Any chance you have a spare men's uniform from facilities that you could lend me for a week or so? A friend has an acting role that calls for a gray uniform."

"Hmm. I don't see why not. Go look in that pile over there and find yourself something in his size. And, Doc, thanks for taking care of my grandbaby a few weeks back. She's my heart. It meant a lot that you personally worked on her case. Appreciate it."

Loud crackles accompanied by metallic gray bolts of lightning zigzagged across the ominous sky as Sydney dashed through the peanut-sized raindrops on her way to purchase a camera, Dustbuster, and large flashlight. After coming back, she dried off, changed, and stashed her goods in the closet.

The light was on in Charles's office. Hearing her enter, he sauntered into her room stopping in front of her desk with his hand on his hip.

"What's up with the ladder?" he asked.

"The beige walls have gotten to me. I'm gonna paint. Your blue color looks so nice."

"Are you going to paint it exactly like mine?" He tilted his head.

"Don't worry. I'm thinking pale green."

"For a wall?"

"I like it."

"You know, those paint fumes are going to really mess up my sinuses. When are you starting?"

"Within the next few days."

"I'm off this weekend if you want to paint."

Charles walked back into his office with a miffed expression and slammed the door.

Twenty-Nine

ATSUKO WAS EXPECTING her when she knocked on the door. She was dressed in a black-and-white Chanel suit. Her long satiny hair flowed down her back as she stood in four-inch spiked black heels. She held open a FedEx overnight pouch. Sydney slipped in the manila envelope from her backpack.

"Let's go," Atsuko said. She headed for the elevator with the package in one hand and an addressed slip in the other.

Sydney stopped. She reached into her backpack again and pulled out a beautifully designed book on Japanese cinema. She tilted her head, bowed it slightly, and, with an extended arm, presented it to Atsuko. "I'd like you to have this. It's one of my favorites, and I thought you might like it too. I'll never forget what you've done for me. Thank you."

"Thank you for lovely book. Not necessary, Sydney-san."

BACK IN HER kitchen, Sydney grabbed a Clorox bottle and a sharp knife. She emptied the solution into a mason jar, rinsed the plastic bottle, and carved an oval seven inches long and three inches wide out of the hard plastic. She dried it and brought it to her front door. She popped the front door lock over and over again. When she opened it in less than five seconds, which took about eight minutes of practice, she stopped.

Thirty

POP. POP. POP. *Pop. Pop.* She shot in a purposeful tight pattern: head, chest, arm, elbow, hand, torso. Switching sides, she ran up and down the body and finished the six preloaded clips she brought from home. Sixty bullets in all—gone. The shoot-up lasted ten minutes. The gunpowder, thick and pungent, hung suspended above her head, filled her nostrils, and she sneezed eight times in rapid succession. After the last bullet was fired, she stood still. Rolling her shoulders, she exhaled. She brought her right arm down to her side, placed the 9mm Beretta on the shelf in front of her, and wiggled her stiff trigger finger. Pleased with her work, she ripped up her paper target.

Sydney looked around the space; it was maybe two by three feet. The walls were painted a dull sandy brown, and the lighting was dreary. This shooting gallery needed Prozac. She heard bullets whoosh by on the left and whiz by on the right. *Pop! Pop!* The ancillary noise was loud and intense even with ear mufflers. It usually distracted her, but not today. Today, she was focused, with laser-slit eyes, a steady arm, and perfect breathing.

Sydney had gone to the gun club from time to time over the past seven years. The owner, Normie, knew her mother from

Chinatown, which was where the original gun club had resided. After trouble with the local gangs, Normie had moved the place to an innocuous block in Midtown. When Sydney joined, Normie welcomed her warmly.

The Hit the Spot Range was hidden in the basement of a nondescript commercial building. Members entered the lobby and walked past a silent doorman to the end of a short, dingy white hallway. They descended a long, twisted staircase that hugged dark olive-green walls plastered with photographs of women arching their backs clad in microshorts and halter tops. At the bottom of the stairwell, there was a typical-looking storefront. From the outside, it could be confused with a hardware store, but once you entered, it was clear that it wasn't True Value. Two men were positioned at the front desk, always. Ammo, high-quality holsters, gun belts, magazine pouches, military clothing, and all sorts of clips were mounted over, under, and around the desk. They hung from nails in wooden planks affixed to beige cement walls.

The desk brigade was usually Normie, a petite and crazy-buff Chinese man close to fifty, and Owen, a similarly built African-American former marine with buckets of charm. When Normie was busy, Chewie, a lanky Chinese fellow whose arms and neck were covered in dragon tattoos, manned the desk.

Normie's club was staffed with knowledgeable workers who were ex-police or ex-military. Normie belonged to the latter group.

The members were a varied bunch. Some were shooters and skilled gunmen who came to practice; a few were disenfranchised folks, ranters who came to blow off steam; and there was a new breed, men and a few women there to learn the art of shooting. Then there was Sydney. She'd held a license for seven years.

The men nodded and stared when Sydney entered. Occasionally, Sydney asked Normie a technical question, but she usually kept to herself and moved straight to a cubicle.

Once the men saw her shoot, they were besotted. She was an enigma. A sure shot with a great eye, steady hand, and cool demeanor. Sharpshooters weren't usually wrapped in bodies like Sydney's, and from the looks on their faces, they were smitten.

She packed her gun and assorted materials and left the shooting area. When she emerged, Normie called out, "How's Ma?"

"The same," she said.

Normie broke into a wide grin.

Thirty-One

SYDNEY CLIMBED THE steps by two, entered the fifth floor, and stopped at the OR desk. She told Phyllis, the woman who staffed it, that she needed to speak to Dr. Inger about a case he'd scheduled. Phyllis's sparkly pink fingernail swiveled the old Rolodex to I, pulled out a card, and handed it to Sydney.

"Knock yourself out, Dr. Chang," she said with a red-lipped grin.

Sydney copied Inger's home address and phone, cell, office, and beeper numbers. As she handed the card back, Phyllis looked at her seriously. "Any word on Dr. Wagner's son?"

"No. May I also look at next week's draft schedule?"

"Sure."

Sydney perused it. *Monday he's off, and Thursday's a super-late day for him.*

Since it was Saturday, Sydney had her office to herself. She dialed.

"Larry? Sydney. You're there! Man, you work 'round the clock. I'm wondering if I can run down again?"

"Twice in one week, Sydney! I'm thrilled. Come on down."

"Give me an hour or two. Is that okay?"

"I'll be waiting."

Gloved, she reached into her bottom desk drawer and retrieved Inger's glove-mask-gum assembly and one of the glassine envelopes containing a piece of the condom. Using a sterile tweezer, she put the gum into a new clean glassine envelope. Next, she shook the soiled condom onto a sterile drape. Dipping the end of a swab into saline until it was damp but not sopping wet, she rubbed it on the condom segment to pick up the DNA contents. The white swab turned a slight burnt reddish-yellow color from the blood-semen mix. When it was sufficiently coated, she rested the stick portion on a different swab at a ninety-degree angle, elevating it so that the specimen tip could dry. She repeated this once more. Finished, she folded and loosely tented the blue drape over the specimens to air-dry.

Opening the ladder, Sydney climbed up to her office's fifteen-foot ceiling. She expected a lot of dust when she popped up a two-by-four-foot white-and-black-dotted ceiling tile. An avalanche of clumped gray dust poured down covering her face, shoulders, and the floor. *Glad I'm wearing scrubs, a hat, and mask. Good thing the specimens are covered.* She scooped out the remaining clumps, jumped off the ladder, and vacuumed.

Up again, she shone her flashlight side to side in the dark, dank space above the ceiling tiles. She estimated that there was about three feet of space from the tiles to the cement top ceiling. *Tight.* Above the aluminum frame that held the tiles was a mix of electrical wires and cables, as well as the housing for the fluorescent lighting fixture that sat above her desk. *Very little wiggle room.* The wires were malleable; the fixture housing was not.

Sydney repositioned the tile and climbed down. Slipping on a pair of sterile gloves, she picked up the now-dry specimen swabs and broke the wooden sticks so that they too fit into a glassine envelope. She placed the envelopes containing the gum and the human fluid swabs into a white letter-sized envelope.

Stripping off her gloves, she pulled out the Clorox cutout and stepped outside of her office into the secretarial area. With the door shut and locked, she slid the cutout into the door groove. *Pop.* Time check. Eight seconds. She walked through her office to Charles's door. Same procedure, seven seconds. Sydney smiled at the thought of Charles seeing her pop his door open.

Thirty-Two

LARRY'S FACE LIT up when she pushed the lab door open.

"I have another question for you," she said. "My mom asked me to do a favor for her friend. It sounds a bit strange."

"Hit me." Larry trailed his small right hand over his gray-speckled goatee.

"My mom's friend thinks her daughter's husband is stealing money out of her bedroom floor safe."

"Okay." His index finger rested on his lips as he looked intently at Sydney.

"So she rigged her safe so that the handle has a sharp edge. If you don't know about it, you'll get cut. Last week she noticed a bit of red on the edge when he was visiting. She immediately called my mom. My mom looked it up on the Internet, and it said to take a cotton swab, swipe it across the red spot, and put it in a baggie. It went on to say that you should get a straw or chewed gum from the person of interest, in this case the woman's son-in-law. So she offered him a piece of gum and then retrieved it when he tossed it. Since I'm the only doctor they can tell this insane story to, I'm elected. They want to get it DNA matched, and they want me to get it done for them."

"Ha! Those ladies are some sleuths."

"Right? She's my mom's best friend for over fifty years, and when they get together, it's always trouble. Any idea who can do this for me? I mean, how can I go about doing this without spending a fortune and having any of our names attached to it? It's a bit out there, even for them."

"Give it to me, Syd. I'll take care of it. I'll have it back to you in a few days."

"Really, Larry? I didn't mean for you to do this personally; I thought you could just direct me…."

When Sydney returned with the package, Larry said, "I'll call you when I have the results."

"'Sydney Weinstein' is starting to sound better and better," she said.

"Just let me know what cut you want on the diamond."

BACK IN HER office, she dialed Hasina. "Anything?"

"Nothing, Sydney. Nothing. Why were you late that morning? You're never late."

Thirty-Three

Home, Sydney pulled out two creased road maps from her bedroom drawer. After plotting a course, she grabbed her helmet and tank bag. It was blisteringly hot at six P.M., as she sped up Park Avenue South on her red Ducati motorcycle. *Glad I didn't find a tracker on my bike.* She hung a right on Twenty-Third Street and a left onto the ramp toward the FDR Drive. Sydney had never visited Greenwich, Connecticut—a community that sat on the Long Island Sound—but she worked with many doctors who lived there. Just thirty-six miles out of Manhattan, they told her it offered everything from great schools to gorgeous beaches.

Past Sixty-First Street and the Ed Koch Queensboro Bridge, at around Seventieth Street, she spotted her first camera. It was affixed to the cement ceiling of the underpass. At Ninety-Sixth Street, the traffic unclogged, and she zipped up to the Willis Avenue Bridge, choosing it to avoid tolls and tracking. Erratic drivers made her search for other cameras difficult; she was forced to focus on the road. Her objective was to determine where the authorities were able to track and where they weren't. It was hard to believe that the professionals were unable to locate the car that had whisked Robbie away.

Fifty minutes later, on the Hutchinson River Parkway, a soft, cooler breeze blew onto her neck. It was two weeks since she'd last ridden, and she missed it. She'd been a rider since eight years old—first minis, then motorcycles, dirt and street—and this Ducati was by far her favorite.

Miles of rich greenery lined the parkway in New York, but when the Hutchinson turned into the Merritt Parkway in Greenwich, it became spectacular—smooth black paved roads, oversized green-and-white signage with a well-designed font. A robust forest hugged it. Her bike glided along this heavenly path, also known as Route 15, until she exited at 31 onto North Street, a main Greenwich thoroughfare.

She rode to Greenwich Point Park, a jutting peninsula located in Old Greenwich, directly on the Long Island Sound. At the small glass admissions booth she paid a sandy-haired teenage boy and slowly entered the parking lot. One side of the park had the cleanest sand Sydney had ever seen. It was accompanied by tranquil water. A few mothers and kids were still building sand castles. The other side had mounds of sparkling crystalline mineralized rocks. They glittered beside the dirt paths that looped around the water and through the meandering woods. Several folks were getting in early evening runs. Sydney rode over to a quiet and secluded area of the lot.

Peeling three small decals of lightning graphics off a roll in her backpack, she affixed them to her helmet. Electrician's tape was used to alter two numbers on her license plate. Two removable decals from another roll, a purple dragon and white wild horses, she stuck on the body of the tank. Securing the full-faced helmet on her head, she pulled on a jean jacket and slipped her hands into dark gloves. As dusk fell, Sydney weaved her way back to the heart of Greenwich, considered one of the five richest communities in the country.

She rode past waterways, idyllic meadows, and enclaves of shaded forests. It was clear that when a buyer moved here, they chose much more than a large house; they bought into a quiet and privileged society, a segregated environment that stood alone in its rarefied uniqueness. They purchased prestige.

Back on other side of North Street, she turned onto Lower Cross Road. *Wow. Inger has done well. Think he grew up poor too.* Drivers cruised by in late-model Lexuses, Mercedes, Bentleys, and she even spotted a Maybach. Then she saw it: a softly lit, engraved wooden sign in front of a tree-lined driveway: INGER #62. A bluebird was perched above the number.

Like many others, Inger's home was a sprawling stone mansion. While most looked classic and old-world, Inger's had a modern twist, a state-of-the-art sensibility.

Warm, ocher-hued lights streamed out of a row of contemporary bay windows, and a solar panel took up a sizable portion of the roof. Two moving cameras monitored the driveway entrance, as was the case with most of the dwellings in the neighborhood. Sydney assumed that if equipment was posted as soon as you entered, chances were high that the entire property was wired. With the houses so close to each other and the intense security, Inger's home was out of the question. So was the hospital parking garage—too much foot traffic. If she chose to have a discussion with him, she needed to find a more secluded location.

She circled back and rode out of Greenwich, Connecticut. Forty-nine minutes later she swerved off the Taconic Parkway in New York, drove a mile east, checked for the old trail, and tore into dense, dark woods.

Thirty-four

SYDNEY FELT JOHNNY's eyes on her the moment she rode onto his land using the camouflaged trail off the two-lane highway. It was a remnant of the narrow path that they'd carved out biking and hiking through its green tangled thickness during their childhood years. She wondered where he was and how he was viewing her. Was it on a handheld device in some distant fancy bar or in town on a grocery store line? Or maybe he was at home on his computer just a few yards away in the middle of their youthful playground—a picturesque woodland that he now owned. The last news Sydney had heard about Johnny came from Lily. Chrissy, his sister, told Lily that he'd invented some major security software program and sold it to a Fortune 500 company. Sounded reasonable since he'd always been building something growing up: robots, go-karts, minibikes… and the things he'd built for her.

Sydney listened for gunshots. She knew there was a slight chance she'd been seen as some errant intruder as she'd ducked branches and pushed her way into the shadowy woods. But that thought quickly vanished—she was pretty sure that her old friend recognized her chosen route and unique riding style. She lay almost flat on the gas tank below the handlebars as her knees bent slightly and her butt jutted out in an extended C curve. Sydney imagined his lips curling on the right side of his small mouth, forming a side grin. He knew.

She drove fast; a bright beam streamed from her headlight as she cut through the thicket of bushes and towering trees on a path overgrown with wild vegetation. Branches slashed at her sleeves and ripped through her paper-thin cotton pants. Bugs dove headfirst into her helmet shield as her bike slid, skidded, and penetrated the forest. She flew past no trespassing, private property signs every few feet, posted on red oaks, black cherries, and sugar maples. Her eyes blinked from occasional glints of moonlight reflecting off of the metal camera casings mounted high in this verdant oasis.

It was twelve years since she'd left, five since they'd last spoken. He became increasingly uncommunicative as she mentioned new friends and activities. She always invited him along, but he declined every time. He asked, "When are you coming to the country?" Sydney remembered their last conversation as stilted. She kept an eye out for wires. She knew he'd have it completely connected, and she wasn't keen on getting jolted with electricity.

Fourteen minutes in, she saw the rock. She stopped the bike and dismounted. Lifting her helmet, she rested it on the leather seat. Rivulets of sweat poured from her temples. She grabbed the neon blue titanium water bottle from her tank pack and walked over to the eleven-foot-high boulder—the boulder that had served as their "headquarters" for nine years, with four large "steps" hidden in strategic holes. She climbed up and sat on its flat, wide, smooth surface. The air smelled sweet. Her ears tingled with the familiar harmonious vocalizations emanating from eastern screech owls and crickets. It was still, but not quiet. She closed her eyes and exhaled fully through her mouth, then inhaled slowly through her nose and blew out again. Her nostrils filled with the memorable scents of her childhood: a youthful eternity spent in companionable silence, fifteen hours a day, as they played, hunted, and explored in the woods.

After a while, she spoke softly into open space: "Johnny, I don't know where you are, but I know you know I'm here. I need my stuff."

Sydney shifted into the lotus posture, closed her eyes, and rested her hands in an open position on the tops of her knees. She breathed in again through her nose and exhaled more slowly through O-shaped, full lips. Ten in. Ten out. *Would this have happened if I hadn't been late that morning? And Hasina—what was she thinking when she let Robbie walk alone in the hospital at that hour? Let it go. Just let it go—like when someone crashes on the OR table. Breathe. Focus. Do. I'm not paid to feel. Just fix.*

Thirty-five

SYDNEY CHANG AND Johnny Russo met when Sydney's parents bought a summer country home across the street from where Johnny's family lived year-round. They purchased it so that Sydney could run around and blow off steam. She was a city kid. Johnny was a townie, a country kid—half-Irish, half-Italian—with three older sisters, an alcoholic mother, and a runaround father.

He was white blond and petite, with a stutter and a slight lisp. By age six, Sydney stood five feet tall with arms that reached her kneecaps, size-nine shoes, a wild head of uncombed dark brown frizz, and a boatload of aggression. A few days after they arrived, Mrs. Russo said to Sydney, "The girls have plenty of friends. Johnny has none. He needs one, and it's you."

Oddly enough, they bonded. They knew nothing about each other's school lives—only that they were in the same grade despite a two-year age difference.

Sydney's back was erect as she sat cross-legged. She ignored the blood-streaked rips up and down her arms caused by the knifelike branches that had torn through her shirt, creating an open all-night feast for bloodthirsty mosquitoes. She waited.

Settling into her pose, her mind traveled. She was thirteen; he was fifteen. One day, Johnny didn't show up at the bus stop where he usually met her on Friday afternoons. She looked for him in the usual places. Kids were running toward the lake park in back of the bus depot. Sydney followed, figuring that he was there. "FIGHT! FIGHT!" they were shouting. She made her way through the crowd, scanned left and right, but didn't see him. When she got to the front, she did. On the ground. Shaking. Four boys surrounded him, kicking and taunting. "Stop. Right this instant," she said in a low and menacing monotone.

The beefiest of the crew, a kid with beady eyes, a bulbous red nose, and a sweaty pug face, paused and eyed Sydney. "Shut the fuck up, nigger."

Sydney snapped her right foot up and into the center of his throat. He dropped. She extended her hand, Johnny grabbed it, and she yanked him up onto his feet. They stood back to back as she dispatched two other boys with a couple of swift kicks to the chest and chin. They could dish it out, but they sure couldn't take it. Wai Sook had taught her well. He'd be proud. One bully was left standing—the biggest. She looked at Johnny and nodded.

"Now it's a fight," she said. They slugged it out. Minutes later, when Johnny hit the ground, she walked over to him and jerked him up.

"It's over; nothing to see here. Take your friends and get lost," she said with her back to the crowd.

She heard rapid footsteps advancing. She could feel the breeze. She looked under her right arm just as a hairy, muscular arm shot past her left cheek. She grabbed it and flipped him hard to the ground, facedown. Placing her knee on the base of his neck, she grabbed a fistful of hair and wrenched his head back.

"Next time I'll snap it," she said into his ear.

They walked away—Johnny with a limp. After a few moments of silence, he spoke. "Syd?"

"Yeah."

"I got some science homework tonight."

"Ugh. How much?"

"I don't know. A lot, I think."

"Okay. I'll do that first, and then we'll start."

Sydney opened her eyes. By the moon's position, she estimated that three hours had passed since she'd arrived.

"Johnny, I know it's been a long time, but I'd like my stuff if you still have it. Would you leave it here for me? I'd appreciate it. I'll be back tomorrow evening. Night."

Thirty-Six

SYDNEY OPENED HER bottom office desk drawer and pulled out a small brown paper bag stamped with a witch's face. It was around three A.M., Sunday. She laid out a few paper towels then removed spirit gum, black crepe, some Q-tips, a scissor, and a tweezer. She pulled out a chipped one-inch-square drugstore hand mirror and an Ace bandage from her backpack. Scissor in hand, she cut the crepe into half-centimeter-wide slivers, three-quarters of an inch in length. When she had a healthy four-inch pile, she opened the spirit gum and poured a few drops into its white cap. She dipped a Q-tip into the sticky solution until soaked. Propping the mirror against a heavy medical tome on her desk, Sydney peered into it and ran the cotton swab over her upper lip and along the sides of her face. With her index finger, she gently touched the areas to make sure that they were sticky. Satisfied, she picked up her first individual sliver of black crepe with the tweezer. She lifted, pressed, and pasted slowly and methodically until a thick and fluffy mustache and sideburns appeared.

Sydney stood in a sleeveless white tank and wrapped the Ace bandage around and around her breasts until they were flattened. It was tight, but she could still breathe. She slipped on the baggy gray uniform top. With a baseball cap on her head, she sank her feet into worn black sneakers and her hands into a thick pair of beige workmen's gloves. Dorky, square, black-framed eyeglasses completed the look. She sauntered into Charles's office and closed the door. In his full-length mirror, she took a quick look. *Goth girl in the costume store knew her stuff.* She grabbed the ladder off of her office floor and picked up the canvas workbag, which held a small digital camera, Dustbuster, flashlight, pen, and notepad. Hunched over as a well-groomed male with a ladder under his arm, a slight limp, and red stitching on the left shirt pocket that read FACILITIES DEPARTMENT, she exited.

The hallway outside of Inger's office was eerily quiet. A cold metallic breeze blew overhead from a nearby vent positioned above the entrance to his outer office door. Her nose twitched. *Don't sneeze. Mustache pieces may fly off. Hold it.* She reached into her right pant pocket, palmed the cutout, then slipped it into the doorjamb. Inside, she shoved a rolled, sausage-shaped towel against the bottom gap of the closed door. She whizzed through the dark secretarial area, looking for potential hiding spots in case she needed one—none. Over to Inger's office door—*pop*, she was in. The lights flicked on automatically; she shut them off. Inger's office was cold, and she shivered as she fired off a series of flashless camera shots of the window area, backlit by the office lights from the facing buildings. She lowered and closed his blinds then switched on the lights in both the office and its outer space. After a few more photos of the window from the outer office, she carried the ladder, pushed the equipment into Inger's room with her foot, and closed the door. Furniture, door positioning, ceilings, bookcases, desks, and file cabinets were shot from multiple angles. She yanked Inger's unlocked top desk drawer open. It was stuffed with receipts from Starbucks, Wings Delite, and Le Pain Quotidien. Spreading them out, she photographed them.

Sydney was pleased to see that the ceiling's height was around thirteen feet, two feet lower than hers. Up top, she slid out two ceiling tiles, and several fist-sized clumps of dark gray dust plopped out. It was roomier than hers, and there was about a foot more space between the filthy tiles and the gray cement ceiling. *Good.* She shot photos from every angle, cleaned up, then repeated the process in the secretarial office and took one last sweeping look around. Sydney turned off the light and opened the blinds. As she shut Inger's door, she slipped her gloved hand through the crack and flipped the light back on.

Thirty-Seven

AN OWL HOOTED. It woke her with a start. She was disoriented for a moment but soon realized that she was on the rock. She estimated that it was around midnight. Rubbing her eyes, she cleared her throat. Straight ahead she spotted an object hanging from a tree. In the moonlight, she couldn't make out what it was but knew it wasn't from nature. She climbed down and moved toward it. It was an old beaten-up burlap sack. Her sack. She jumped up and grabbed it.

On the ground, she released the drawstring and pulled out an expandable metal stick, a custom-made crossbow, three arrows, a throwing knife, two blow darts, a blowpipe, two throwing stars, specialty handheld pitons, and an animal tranquilizer gun. She beamed.

Sensing something, she swiveled on her butt, and there he was, standing in front of her, hands clasped calmly behind his back. "Thank you," she said, looking into his eyes.

"No problem."

Chirps and buzzes filled the air as Sydney examined each item thoroughly. Several minutes later, he spoke. "Lily, again?"

"She's in trouble, like always, but this isn't about her. A little boy I know has been missing for almost a week, and the authorities have come up empty so far. I have a possible lead that requires some, let's say unconventional, tactics to exploit."

Sydney peered up at him. "How've you been?"

"Alive."

Sydney lifted a throwing star and showed it to him. "Everything's in pristine condition. That's great. Thanks again."

He nodded. "Tell me what else you need me to do."

"It'll be illegal and potentially dangerous."

"Okay," he said.

"Are you sure? Because it's a lot."

He tilted his head to the right; his shoulder-length hair moved in concert. His chest and biceps were noticeably larger—his thighs, too—and his hair was still white blond.

"Well, I'll need two small motion-triggered video cameras with large memory cards. Also, I'll need a dart rifle with a fiber-optic end scope and fillable tranquilizer rounds. Some expandable stilts, three detonators, a stiletto knife, two expandable batons, and burner phones. I'll need at least four phones, some trackers that stick on a car and can be removed by remote, and appliqués that will adhere to license plates requiring no skill to place." She grinned. "Well, you asked."

"Give me two days for most of it, an extra to finish everything," he said. "Oh, and with the phones. I'll remove the secondary batteries, but never use them at home or in any location you don't want tracked to you. Make sure you keep the battery and SIM card out until right before you use them, then destroy and toss the SIMs and remove the batteries."

Sydney placed her equipment back in the sack and handed it to him. She threw her leg over the bike, mounted it, and positioned her helmet.

"Johnny. Thanks."

Johnny stood in place, his hands dug into his front jean pockets. His white T-shirt blew slightly around the bottom seam, his head pointed to the ground, and his eyes lifted up, watching her.

She switched on the ignition, watching him in her back mirror as she drove away. *Some people never change. Man, am I lucky.*

Thirty-Eight

THE MOMENT BEFORE checking the message, she held her breath. The solitary red light blinked in the dark room as Sydney walked into her office around seven Tuesday morning. *Maybe they found him.* She had the same thought every time she saw the voice-mail light. *It's been seven days.*

"Hey, Sydney Weinstein. Larry Weinstein here. I have the results. Stop by; I'm around."

LARRY WAS IN his usual getup—loose faded jeans with baggy knees and a green plaid short-sleeved shirt—when Sydney pushed open the lab door.

"Thanks for doing this so quickly," she said as she placed two white paper bags on the black lab station: one filled with food, the other with canned drinks.

"So, the results. Drumroll, please... The DNA from the swab and gum had at least one ninety-nine-point-nine percent match. Looks like your mom's friend just found the culprit."

The muscles in Sydney's face tightened. Her left eye squinted, opened, and closed.

"Isn't that good news?" Larry asked as his red-haired head pitched forward and tilted right.

"Yes and no." Then Sydney paused. "Now the craziness begins," she said with a slight smile. "Larry, thanks a ton."

"Hey, stay a minute and share some of the food you brought me. I can't possibly eat—let's see—three bagel sandwiches and two cookies all by myself," he said as he rummaged through the bags.

"Of course," she said sitting down. She exhaled. *Okay, it's Inger's condom. But does it have anything to do with Robbie?*

"Lox and cream cheese, tuna, or egg, bacon, and cheese?" he asked.

"You do eat bacon, right?"

"My family gorges on bacon. We're good Jews."

"Funny. I'll have the tuna."

Larry dove into the overstuffed egg sandwich with relish. Sydney chewed silently.

"I don't mean to be nosy, Sydney, but isn't this the outcome your mom's friend wanted? She's probably not happy that her son-in-law is stealing, but at least she'll feel less like a looney tune."

"I guess. But now they're going to be uncontrollable."

Thirty-Nine

"Syd, I need to tell you something important. Really important," Lily's voice bellowed.

"I'm sleeping. Do you realize it's four fourteen A.M., Lily? What's so important?" Sydney yawned.

"You know I'm good with makeup, right?"

If you like the Goth look 24/7.

"And I'm even better since my funereal experience, right? Well, they were talking about Robbie on the news last night, and I saw a photo of the blond woman and the boy. The woman is a total fake, Syd. A total fake. She has built-out cheekbones with a bogus chin, and she's definitely wearing a wig. I'm not even sure if it's a woman. I wanted you to know in case it helps. So if the detectives are looking for a blond woman, they may be wasting a lot of time. That's all I wanted to tell you. Okay, bye."

As soon as she got to work, Sydney rifled through her office desk and found the detective's card.

"Hi, Detective. It's Sydney Chang. I wanted to pass along some information that might be helpful. A hair and makeup professional I know saw Robbie's video on television and thought that the blond woman's appearance was a complete cosmetic alteration. You probably know that already, but just in case, I thought I'd call."

"We know, Dr. Chang. Thanks."

"Any closer?"

"We're working on it."

WHEN SYDNEY ARRIVED home, she saw a note stuffed into her doorjamb. Her heart pounded.

> Sydney, knock on door. No problem what time.
> *Atsuko.*

Atsuko greeted her with an ethereal smile.

"I have all information." She unlocked a desk drawer and took out a large white envelope with Japanese writing on it. Atsuko handed it to her.

"I did best I could. I do not know all words, some medicine words I do not know, you understand," she said, eyes fixed on Sydney's face.

"I'm sure I can figure it out. Atsuko, I'll never forget this. Thanks. Please tell me how much I owe you."

"Oh, no. It is fine, Sydney," she said with a sad smile and a wave of her hand. "I hope it helps. I hope everything okay." Atsuko cast her eyes down. She walked Sydney to the door, opened it, and bowed deeply.

"Be careful, Sydney-san," she whispered.

SITTING ON THE floor of her entranceway, Sydney ripped opened the envelope.

RESULTS
Mixed Specimen: Blood, Sperm, and Epithelial
    Cells

Telomere length measure: TRF length using TeloTAGGG telomere length assay by Southern blot.

DNA PATTERN: BLOOD
Male
Leukocyte telomere length consistent with an age of six, plus or minus four years.

DNA PATTERN: SPERM
Male
Donor age indeterminable.

Acrid bile rushed up, flooding Sydney's throat. She now knew that there was a pedophile in the hospital—at least one, Inger. She knew the abused child was not Robbie because the timing was wrong. *So who is the child? And is it linked to Robbie's kidnapping?*

Forty

THE HEADLIGHT BOUNCED with rays of light ricocheting off of the trees as the motorcycle pushed its way back into the forest. Sydney removed her helmet and spotted a wisp of snowy hair right before he emerged from a small opening in the woods.

"I have something to show you," she announced, dismounting. Johnny motioned her to follow, and in silence, they entered a narrow footpath. Branches swiped their thighs, leaves crunched under their feet, and a fragrant sweetness permeated the air. His hair was brushed back, worn loose. It softly touched the top of his wide shoulders, forming a gentle flip as it swung and glistened in the moonlight. Her eyes moved to his strong, bare feet—they reminded her of well-worn, sun-bleached moccasins. Her own feet had softened after her mother insisted that she wear shoes in the city from the sixth grade on. She threatened, "Sydney, no shoes, no grape juice." The risk of no grape juice, the only liquid Sydney drank, had done the job. Since she knew that she had no means of earning her own money in the sixth grade, she'd slipped into beat-up sneakers.

They exited the dense forest into a clearing. A groomed lawn with a rectangular log house appeared. The roof was covered with solar panels; the structure had a hand-worked façade—each log created a utilitarian yet highly artistic design. The inside was interesting too; the walls were curved and uniquely shaped. The great room occupied the middle of the house. A bedroom, a study, a kitchen with stainless steel appliances, and a sea-green-glass-tiled bathroom jutted off the central room like spokes on a wheel. Johnny's home was rustic on the outside and spotlessly space-age on the inside, with gleaming blond wood floors and white walls. Sydney liked it.

They moved in silence, like the old days. Sydney followed him into the study, where he bent down and folded back about six inches of a five-foot circular plush gray carpet, exposing a recessed metal handle. He hoisted it and lifted a carpet-covered circular trapdoor. A humming gust of arctic air punctuated by intermittent pings filled the study. Johnny descended, disappearing. Sydney peered in, then climbed down the slim, metal fourteen-foot-long ladder. As her head cleared the opening, Johnny pulled an attached chain. A thump, a breeze, and the door snapped shut.

They were in a brightly lit narrow room that ran the length of the house. A wall covered with screens flashed colorful, continuously changing information. A central station faced the screens, housing keyboards and banks of computer central processing units. Off to the side, in a corner behind glass, sat a workstation neatly filled with a variety of metal and plastic widgets, wiring, and hand tools. Sydney was surprised at how tiny the work area was.

Johnny motioned her over to two gray mesh high-backed chairs in front of a *Star Wars*-like yellow, green, and red blinking display panel. She placed the camera in his hand. He downloaded and projected a myriad of photos onto an oversized screen. Sydney explained her plan to question Inger. He listened. When she was through, he said, "It would be faster with two people."

"I'll do it alone. Let's start. Nice job building the house."

With his lips together, he smiled. Then his brow furrowed.

"You know, Syd, if this guy, Inger, gets spooked and calls his john, and let's say the pimp actually has the boy, he'll just get rid of him. It's the easiest way to cover his tracks."

"I know. I'm taking that into account. Oh, Robbie's his name."

They sat side by side in front of the computer. He handed her a bottle of ice-cold purple grape juice. Johnny suggested options; she shook her head yes or no, adding additional insights and ideas. It was the grown-up version of the hide, seek, and ambush games that they used to play in the forest—no more dangerous, just different.

By twelve thirty, the logistics of the first phase were complete. Johnny stopped in front of the back wall of his workshop. With his tanned thumb and index finger on the wall, he slid it open. She grinned. Johnny climbed in, pivoted, and offered his hand. She accepted it and stepped into the dark and damp stone passageway. It was cold and wet as they marched uphill about sixteen yards, by her estimate, surfacing through a grass-covered manhole in the forest. The house was barely visible. She knew Johnny would have an emergency exit, an escape tunnel. He always did.

Johnny handed over the rest of the equipment, item by item. She opened and inspected every phenomenally crafted piece. His equipment designs always awed. When a rare, errant screw wasn't seated precisely or a part didn't open with ease, he tweaked it on the spot.

Sydney walked off into the night. The evening air was humid with a pleasant breeze. She searched for a target. The oak tree on the far side would do. She approached it with a spray can and painted a white circle, approximately seven inches in diameter, smack in the middle of its trunk. With just enough moonlight for illumination, she began. When she was young, this was second nature. Now it took all of her concentration as she focused on her target from every angle, upright to supine, and in every state of motion, stationary to jumping. She used all of the weapons in the bag except the blowpipe; she didn't want to leave a potential DNA trace. When she hit the spot dead center with consistency, feeling as fluid as she did when she was twelve, she stopped.

Sydney pulled out two new metal stilts with interlocking sliding segments, enabling expandability. Each had two footpads: one for the ground and one for a foot. She slipped her feet onto the footpads, strapped them in, and stood.

Two hours later, muddied, she jogged out of the woods on stilts, rounded back to the house, and found Johnny outside with a block of concrete the size of a dishwasher. He handed her a drill and a bag filled with lag shields, hook screws, and carabiners.

She practiced about twenty minutes, until she consistently set four lag shields into the concrete, spaced into the configuration they had plotted, in less than four minutes.

"Strong work, Syd," he said. "I want to show you one last thing."

Gravel crunched under their feet. About seven minutes later, they entered a clearing with two large, side-by-side, freestanding structures. Johnny pressed two buttons on his cell phone, and the metal garage doors lifted, with bright light pouring out. A Dodge RAM truck, a red 1969 Mustang in mint condition, and three motorcycles—a Honda off-road, a Ducati sports bike, and a custom chopped Harley sparkled in one building. The other was a spectacular work shed filled with rows of power tools dangling from metal wall hooks, teak built-in units, and dozens of blinking machines hooked up to computers.

"Wow," she said.

Now she understood why the work area in the cellar was so small. It was a satellite.

WATER STREAMED DOWN her face and body as she soaped up with castile soap in a gleaming glass-and-metal shower. The bathroom door creaked open. She stopped lathering, waiting in the foggy stall. Johnny threw a towel, T-shirt, and gym shorts onto the vanity and left. She rinsed, dried off, and slipped on the clean-smelling, vintage Guns N' Roses shirt and blue gym shorts.

Sydney dozed off on the bedsheets that he'd arranged on the icy blue suede living room couch. Then her eyes popped open. She looked around for Johnny. From her vantage point, she couldn't see him. A dim light streamed out of the study, and she heard rustling. They were back to their old pattern—Sydney conking out, Johnny tinkering through the night. She fell back to sleep.

Sydney's watch beeped. It was five A.M. and dark. She dragged her body from the couch as Johnny approached with a mug of steaming coffee, light with cream, just the way she liked it. Although the screened front windows were open, the space was silent. The forest's inhabitants were still asleep.

"Another?" he asked. She shook her head no.

He handed her a biker's shoulder bag stuffed with gear. "I added a totally clean, untraceable revolver loaded with hollow points."

From the leather side bag on her bike, she pulled out a bulky envelope stuffed with three half-inch-thick packets of $50 and $100 bills. The money was part of her savings, the savings that had begun at fourteen working after school and nights at a Mobil gas station. Even then she'd always put 5 percent of every paycheck away; the rest contributed to the household finances to help support her mother and sister.

"Let me know if that's enough to cover everything."

Johnny placed it underneath his armpit without counting. "It's enough."

Forty-One

THE NEWS COVERAGE *has moved on. Maybe Robbie's case is on the back burner? Crap.*

She knew that Inger's OR day was packed with a few quick operations followed by a Whipple, a complicated, lengthy procedure for pancreatic cancer. If everything else went smoothly, the Whipple was set to start at five thirty; he'd be busy until at least midnight. Around nine P.M., she stood in front of the OR bulletin board and noted Inger's operating room. Looping around, she peeked inside. He was behind schedule and just beginning the en bloc removal of the specimen. He had at least three hours to go. *Perfect.*

Transformed into a handyman again, she entered his office unseen. The lights didn't flicker on automatically, and the blinds were up. She worked in the dark. Stripping off the uniform, she stood in a skintight, full-body, black unitard. A harness that held an intricate rope-and-pulley system was secured around her chest and hips. She slid on night vision goggles, taking care not to disturb the rolled-up sheer stocking covering the top of her head, underneath her cap.

From the side of her pack, she detached the stilts. Sitting on the edge of his desk, she attached each stilt to her foot, ankle, and knee. She extended a two-foot segment, stood, then lowered and locked one segment on the right foot while weighting the left foot, then switched and lowered one on the left, weighting the right. She alternated one leg and one segment at a time until she reached the ceiling tiles.

Sliding two tiles up and out onto the existing framework exposed the cement ceiling. She drilled four separate holes, placed the lag shields, screwed hooks into them, and attached the carabiners. Next, she cut out a one-and-a-half-inch irregular hole in the corner of one of the removed tiles.

Snapping her backpack onto one of the carabiners, she put back the used gear and assembled the custom-built rifle with a fiber-optic cable sight. She loaded a prefilled dart containing the short-acting sedatives remifentanil and ketamine into the rifle, then strapped the firearm onto a carabiner. She needed him awake enough to answer questions accurately, yet drugged and foggy enough to not remember anything or at least to think that he was dreaming.

After securing an orange surgical mask around her mouth and nose, she fastened her shoulder harness and the crossed-over hip harness lines to the carabiners. Hanging, she closed the expandable stilts until the rods attached to the outside of her legs and the pads under her feet were all that remained.

Using the pulley system, she reeled in the harness, elevating her head and shoulders about an inch from the cement ceiling. Tensing her core, she bent her knees into her chest, straightened her legs, and lifted them above the ceiling tiles and aluminum framework. In one smooth motion, she unclipped the crossed ropes, flipping her hips over so that they faced the floor. She moved the ceiling tiles back into their original positions, took the rifle, and sighted the room through the fiber-optic scope. The clock on Inger's desk read

10:49 P.M. as she laid the rifle across the aluminum framework and tiles.

Suspended like Spider-Man, Sydney's hands and legs rested on the metal venting and cold steel pipes. The air was stagnant and thick. She figured that Inger had another hour or two in the OR, so she moved the goggles onto her forehead. She relaxed into the darkness and closed her eyes. She ran through her drug choices again.

A key entered the lock; her eyes popped open. Every inch of her body fired up. It was 12:23 A.M. The lights flipped on.

She peered through the scope of the rifle. Inger walked over to the blinds, looked outside, then closed them. He sat down at his desk. From his drawer, he pulled out a water bottle and some popcorn. Turning on his laptop, he stared at the silent screen. She couldn't see or hear it. She waited. Her main concern was that he'd change out of scrubs into street clothes and leave. It was minutes before one A.M.

He fumbled with the string on his scrub bottoms. She placed her finger on the trigger. This was not the way she'd wanted to take him. He'd remember if she took him down when he was awake. *If he's undressing to leave, I have no choice.* Inger's hand was under the desk as his arm traveled up and down in slow motion. *Really?* Sydney's finger stayed positioned. His movements got faster; his breathing grew thicker. His eyes steadied on the screen as his breaths became quicker, hungrier. He moaned as his arm sped up becoming more determined. His face turned dark red, and he climaxed with a loud guttural groan. His head dangled to the right; he exhaled. From a tissue box on his desk, he plucked a few and wiped off his lap.

He walked over to the closet. Her finger tensed. He reached in, pulling a fresh pair of greens off the shelf. Her finger slid off the trigger. He changed, shut the light off, and lay down on the couch. She exhaled.

Her watch read 1:38 A.M. Inger's breathing pattern was deep and steady. She moved her night vision goggles back down and sighted his forearm. Ping.

Forty-Two

FREEING THE DART from his arm, right next to the puncture site, Sydney inserted an IV, then checked his pulse and respirations. Steady. She started a propofol drip. She hogtied Inger with duct tape over blue cloth OR towels, taped his mouth closed, and repositioned him with his face toward the couch. Her goal was uncomfortable, unbruised immobility. She switched off the drip, injected midazolam, and waited.

His eyelids were heavy, opening slowly. He struggled against the restraints. She leaned up close to the back of his right cheek, whispering into the voice synthesizer positioned near his ear. "You will not struggle or scream. You will listen." He froze.

"Interested parties are concerned that your activities have something to do with the missing boy. There will be no weak links. They like it when things are even. They expect me to even things up," she said.

He was awake and groggy but amnestic. The drug-induced sleep was subsiding, returning his ability to speak. He strained against the ties.

She continued, "You will answer questions after I remove the tape." He fought. "No moving, no noise. First question. State your name."

She was gentle as she took hold of the tab, partially peeling the tape off of his mouth, leaving it attached at one corner. She pressed record.

"Dr. Robert Inger."

"Do you have sex with boys?"

"No," he answered, then paused. "What do you want?"

Sydney retaped his mouth and pressed off on the recorder. She injected succinylcholine. He twitched. Within a minute, he was unable to move or breathe. He was awake and paralyzed. Her gloved finger checked his carotid pulse; it was racing. When the color of his lips changed through her night vision goggles and his pulse started to decrease, signaling deoxygenation, Sydney put a mask over his nose and mouth. She administered positive pressure breaths with an Ambu bag resuscitating him. His facial color returned to normal. He was still paralyzed. In a quiet, monotone, synthesized voice, she stated, "I'm only going to ask each question once."

His beeper chirped. She read the text.

> Please come assess patient abdominal pain in emergency room space six. Thanks, Brian Reynolds.

She put it on vibrate only. Inger pulled against his restraints. *In about twenty minutes, Brian, or some other resident, will call his office phone. If he doesn't get an answer, he'll come.* Sydney waited for him to breathe on his own. She removed the mask, peeled back the tape, and pressed record.

"Do you have sex with young boys?" she asked.

"Yes," he answered.

"What service do you use to find these boys?"

"Chicken," he replied.

"Good-bye," she said and placed her hand on his IV line.

"Wait," he croaked. "I use a chicken service to get the boys."

"Be specific. Names."

"No names. I call a central dispatch number and order chicken. At the end of the order, I say, 'All sauces, extra-extra-spicy, please.'"

"Meaning?"

"I want a boy."

She took a deep breath. She felt a rush of heat course through her body. *Skanky piece of detritus. Breathe. Focus. Do.* "Do you speak to the same person every time?"

The beeper rattled. *The call's next, then they'll show up.*

"Yes."

"How do they know what time you want the boy?"

"It's coded into their system."

"Where are they located?"

"Food trucks."

"Where?"

"All over the city."

"And their name?"

"Wings Delite." *His desk drawer receipts!*

She restarted the propofol drip to keep Inger asleep and breathing. Two minutes later she cut the tape and towels, repacked her bag, and checked to make sure that she had everything. *Floor clean. Check.*

With her uniform and disguise in place, she carefully pulled the tape off Inger's mouth. From her pants pocket, she removed a plastic bag, retrieving a cotton pad presoaked in adhesive remover. She wiped his mouth. She plucked out another cotton pad, this one soaked with water, and washed off any taste that may have remained.

Sydney gave Inger an extra bolus of propofol, then removed the IV from his vein. She shoved the IV gear into a plastic bag in her backpack. She grabbed the ceramic table lamp that sat next to the couch and slammed it into his arm in the exact spot from which she'd removed the IV. It caused several abrasions and camouflaged the needle hole. She dropped the lamp on the floor and watched it shatter. She yanked off the goggles, rolled up the face mask, and stuffed them into her bag. She pulled her cap onto her head. With her bulging backpack in place and hands still gloved, she turned the knob of Inger's door. She heard a loud knock on the outer office door. *He didn't call; he just came.*

"Dr. Inger?" he called out. "Dr. Inger, it's Brian Reynolds. Are you okay? I beeped you."

She heard the doorknob wiggle. "Dr. Inger? Hello?"

She figured that she had five, maybe six minutes tops before Inger awoke. She exited his office and positioned herself behind the door in the outer secretary office. She quietly reached into her backpack and snapped the fiber-optic scope off of the rifle barrel.

"Dr. Inger, I'm going to get the master key. Hang on," Brian called.

Sydney waited an extra minute then placed the fiber-optic tip under the door. Clear: no feet. She slipped out with the sound of Inger's loud snores in the background.

Forty-Three

NEW YORK CITY police commissioner Ryan Mahoney was holding an early morning press conference. Sydney was getting dressed for work and flicked on the television just as he was about to speak.

"After an extensive and relentless search for young Robbie Wagner, who disappeared on the Upper East Side ten days ago, both the New York City Police Department and the FBI are continuing to look for new leads and any information that can shed light on his whereabouts. We're asking all New Yorkers to stay vigilant and keep their eyes and ears open for any signs. No matter how small, or odd, in your neighborhood, at your place of work, at the train station if anything is out of order, please call the eight hundred number posted below. This number will stay in operation twenty-four-seven as we continue to search for Robbie. The more eyes on this, the better chance we have of finding him. Thank you."

They're out of leads? How is it possible that they came up empty? The ring must be tight and professional. Was the chicken truck vetted and cleared? I'll follow my lead. If I give it to them and they blow it, I can't pursue it.

An hour later, she was looking for the chicken truck around the block from the hospital. It wasn't there. In her outer office, two zaftig secretaries were finishing powdered jelly donuts when she entered.

"Hey, ladies. Have you ever ordered from the Wings Delite truck out front?" The women looked at Sydney, then at each other, and laughed.

"Eat there?" Alma said. "I love that truck! Don't you see my bags? I'm there three, four times a week. Best chicken wings evah."

Alma's office mate, Juney, chimed in, "Uh-huh." They air-high-fived each other.

"You need to get you some today, Dr. Chang. They are mm-mm good," Juney said as she wiped the dotted powder from her orange-stained lips and sipped coffee from a mug imprinted with a little boy's smiling face.

"What time does the truck show up? I'm already hungry," Sydney said.

"Every day at eleven. Get there early, cuz there's always a line."

At eleven, Sydney dialed the number on a Wings Delite receipt. She was taken aback when she heard the voice of a middle-aged man. Whenever she ordered in from McDonald's, the operators sounded like teenagers.

"Hi, just wondering what your hours are today?" she asked.

"Same as every day, miss. Eleven A.M. 'til four P.M., Monday through Friday."

"Great. And how long a wait is it usually?"

"If you order by phone or Internet, you can go by the truck fifteen minutes later and pick it up. If you stand on line, depending on which truck you're at, it can be five to twenty-five minutes."

"And where are the truck stops?"

"Sixth and Fifty-Second, First and Eighty-Sixth, and Gold Street in the Financial District. Would you like to order?"

"I'm not sure what I want. I'll stop by a truck."

It was another light summer workday, and Sydney was on line by early afternoon. Twelve minutes later, she reached the front, ordering a fried chicken plate with coleslaw and double-fried French fries. As they lifted the chicken out of the fryer with tongs, jiggled the fries into white paper cones, and scooped out the slaw, Sydney inquired how she could order by phone. The young server, with a retro beehive and a badge that read RUBY, told her to call the central number.

"Is that a reliable way to order? You have so many trucks. Don't you ever confuse things and send orders to the wrong location?"

Ruby laughed. "Never happens. The boss takes the orders. He gets it right."

Sydney smiled. "My sister's looking for a job. I think this would be fun for her. Should she call your boss?"

"No. That number is only for orders. Mr. Fenly doesn't do the hiring anymore. He's too busy on the phones. Tell your sister to call the main office. 800-244-1600. Ask for Miriam."

"And Miriam is...?"

"The boss's wife, and now she does the hiring."

"Great. Would she interview in Manhattan?"

"Queens."

"I'll tell her. Can't wait to dig in. These look amazing."

"They are."

And so they were, but the situation sucked the delight out of each soy-soaked, crispy bite.

AT HOME, SYDNEY changed into a dark, oversized, long-sleeved shirt and loose pants then grabbed a helmet and brown biker gloves. She rode back uptown on her motorcycle with a case camouflaging the gas tank and an altered license plate. The traffic picked up as rush hour kicked in. She parked on the corner of East Eighty-Fifth Street, a block away from the truck. Through her helmet's black-tinted face shield, she watched it close for the day. Once the serving shelf was cleared and cleaned, the rolling metal awning came down, and the male server and Ruby got into the cab of the truck. Sydney cranked the engine and followed.

They entered Queens from the Fifty-Ninth Street Bridge and continued another few miles down quiet, tree-lined streets until they pulled into a dead-end alley on a deserted block. There was a parking lot with a two-story nondescript gray building on the far end and the East River in the distance. The truck pulled into a spot next to another Wings Delite truck and a few cars. Sydney rode past, idled her bike on the corner out of sight, and positioned the side mirror to view the lot. When Ruby and her coworker entered the building's steel back door, Sydney rode around the block. The parallel street dead-ended into a well-groomed park. Surveying the area, she realized that she was behind the Pepsi sign that sat in Gantry Plaza State Park in Long Island City, the iconic red script logo she'd driven by on the FDR for years.

After parking her bike on the corner, she strolled back to the chicken lot. Positioned in back of a green garbage bin, she watched two more Wings Delite trucks pull in and drop off workers carrying stacked foil trays. By six o'clock, the trucks were lined up, and a late-model black Cadillac was the only car left in the lot. She leaned against the building's wall.

A man, maybe six two, pushing fifty, with sparse strawberry blond hair, a distended midsection, and a phlegmy cough, emerged with an attaché case around eight P.M. When he entered the Cadillac, Sydney sauntered to the corner, mounted the motorcycle, and waited. The man traveled through the

Midtown Tunnel, then drove over to the West Side Highway. He continued south to Clarkson Street, made a U-turn, and Sydney followed. A few blocks north, he made a right onto West Tenth Street. When a green electric garage door lifted on a narrow brownstone between Washington and Greenwich Streets, he pulled in. Sydney passed him.

He didn't look like the West Village type; he had too much gut, and his slacks looked like a polyester blend. A plaid short-sleeved shirt and shiny brown loafers completed the look. Sydney squeezed her bike in between two SUVs on Greenwich Street. Reaching into the tank bag, she pulled out a dark blue baseball cap and sunglasses. She strolled a few feet west to a large cement playground and leaned against its surrounding metal fence. Through the grating, she had a clear view of the front of the town house.

West Tenth Street was a dark, sleepy block paved in cobblestone, giving it an old-world European charm. In the 1970s and '80s, leather bars were located on the extreme west end of the street. Now there was a ritzy private school for grades K–8. Diagonally across from the school sat slim brownstones and an apartment building. On occasion, a resident arrived home by taxi. It was almost ten, and Sydney's eyes were closing. At 10:40 P.M., the town house garage door slowly rose. She stood at attention. The Cadillac pulled out, heading east. At the end of the block it crossed the street and drove into an empty private outdoor parking lot, a square of cement with space for about five cars. He parked and headed back to the house, attaché case in hand.

Minutes later, a deep blue SUV rounded the corner, then pulled into the driveway and straight into the garage. She was able to detect a man in the driver's seat. The door descended. She couldn't see if anyone else was in it. Her neck muscles tightened. *Are there kids in that SUV?*

Five minutes later the garage door opened again, and the SUV drove out. She pushed the cap lower on her forehead, following the car with her eyes. He drove east on Tenth Street and parked in the same lot. He, too, was middle-aged and of medium build and height. With sandy-brown hair parted on the side, he wore nondescript faded jeans and a loose, light-colored T-shirt.

  The moment he entered the town house, she pulled one of Johnny's prepaid burner phones out of her pant pocket. She slipped in a SIM card and battery.

  "Lily?" she whispered.

  "Huh?"

  "Lily. Wake up."

  "What's up?"

  "I need you to get dressed and meet me. Take a cab and I'll pay for it when you arrive. Now."

  "What? Why? I'm asleep. I don't feel well. Can't I meet you tomorrow?"

  "No, Lily. Throw on some shorts and a baseball cap and meet me on the corner of Tenth Street and Greenwich in the West Village. Did you get that?"

  "Where?"

  "Greenwich, corner of Tenth Street. West Village. Just get into a cab and come now, Lily."

  "I feel sick. I, I would, you know, but I have a stomachache and I can't get up."

  "Get into a taxi now. I'm not asking you, Lily. I'll be looking for you to pull up in about ten minutes. Good-bye."

  "But…"

  A few minutes later a battered yellow cab drove up, and Lily swung the door open. Sydney looked in the front window to read the meter and handed the driver six dollars. Sniffing, Lily rolled out. She shuffled on the cement, following Sydney to the edge of the playground.

"What's the emergency?" Lily asked.

"Lower your voice."

"What's the emergency?" she whispered.

"I'm watching the house with the orange door across the street. Over there," she said, tilting her head. "There's a chance they're trafficking kids and it may lead to Robbie. I'm waiting to see if there's any more activity tonight. I'm interested in a particular SUV. If it pulls into the garage and out again, I need you to walk up close to it and see if there are any kids in it. You need to be inconspicuous. Can you do that?"

"I mean, I've never been a spy or anything."

"Lily, no one disappears quicker than you on the street. You become invisible in a second when you need to—just do it."

"Oh. Oh, okay, Syd. Tell me what to do."

"Sit tight until I see the SUV. When I tell you, cross the street and stand on the corner over there. As it drives past, look in. If you see kids, scratch your head. If you don't see any, don't scratch. Either way, cross the street and hail a cab home."

"Okay. Okay." Just then the garage door lifted.

"Lily. Shhhhh. Be quiet. Stay still."

It couldn't have been more than a minute later when a new-model Mercedes rounded the corner and pulled into the garage. The door descended, and so did Sydney's spirits.

"What does that mean, Syd?"

"I don't know yet."

Sydney stood erect; Lily curved onto the fence with her fingers looped inside and around the metal. Lily's head bobbed up and down as she passed in and out of consciousness, using the grating to hold up her frail frame. Sydney nudged Lily's arm and her head jerked up. She handed Lily a stick of red licorice. Lily shoved the whole thing in her mouth and chomped. There was a creak. They looked toward the house.

Nothing. About fifty minutes later, a loud click echoed and the garage door lifted. Sydney gently elbowed her sister.

"Lily, wake up," she whispered. The Mercedes pulled out. Down came the door. The car passed, driven by an older, distinguished-looking man. He headed east on Tenth Street, then made a left onto Greenwich.

It was close to midnight when the SUV driver exited the orange door and strode over to the parking lot. Sydney woke Lily and told her to pull herself together. The driver pulled out. Lily looked at Sydney with a puzzled expression.

"You remember the instructions?" Sydney asked.

"Yeah, yeah. But I don't have any money." Sydney gave Lily a ten for the ride back home and wondered if she'd make it.

The SUV turned the corner, then, as Sydney expected, re-entered the garage, and the door closed.

"Now, Lily. Start to walk. Slowly."

"Okay, okay."

Lily moseyed over and stood slightly hunched. Minutes later the garage door lifted. The SUV drove out, east on Tenth Street. As it turned north on Greenwich, Lily straightened a bit and looked in. After it passed, she crossed Greenwich and hailed a cab.

The Wings Delite man emerged a few short minutes later, coughed his way to the Cadillac, and took off up Greenwich. Sydney kept three cars behind. They traveled back over the Fifty-Ninth Street Bridge and onto Queens Boulevard. A few open diners, some all-night gas stations, and a blast of disco music emanating from a side-street strip joint broke the stillness of the evening as they drove east. Entering Forest Hills, the car drove into a residential area past colonial homes with manicured front lawns. At the end of a leafy block, it pulled into a circular driveway. He ambled down the verdant path, past another Cadillac, and over to the front door. Slipping in a key, the man entered. When the lights in his front yard turned off, Sydney rolled the bike up to the elongated black tin mailbox at the end of the driveway. The sign on top read: THE FENLYS.

On the side of the road right before the Fifty-Ninth Street Bridge, she pulled out a burner phone. She texted Johnny.

> Please check license plate numbers: NY HET 2371, NY FYA 5325, NY DVN 5318; NY GTJ 3946. Syd

Next she texted Lily's boyfriend.

> David, please meet me on 14th and 8th in an hour from now at 2, if u can. Sydney

She removed the battery and SIM card, smashing everything with a rock.

Forty-four

DAVID WAS ON the northeast side of Fourteenth Street, holding a tattered coffee cup, as Sydney rode up. She smiled. Strips of thinning hair plastered his cheeks, camouflaging three-quarters of his unshaven face. His clothes were baggier than usual.

"What's up?" he asked in a booming voice.

"We need to speak quietly. I'd like you and Lily to do some surveillance work for me."

He chuckled. "Seriously, Syd? You're pulling my chain."

"It's about Robbie." Dirty newspaper pieces rustled on the street as the wind uprooted and tossed them flat onto her leg. Turning, she shook it, dislodging them.

"Oh, sorry. Lily told me. Geez. Any word yet?"

"Not yet. I need a big favor David. Can you help me?"

"Sure, Syd."

She pulled a large manila envelope out of her backpack handing it to him. "Inside are five items. First: appliqués to alter your license plate. You have to do that today because I need you and Lily in your car tonight. Second: clear plastic gloves. Next: a walkie-talkie and tracker. Please bring them with you tonight. And finally, there's a stick-on camera. Please walk it over to West Tenth Street now. It's between Greenwich and Washington and look for the orange door: 273½. A flower box is on the window of the town house next door. Peel off the paper and stick the camera on the side of the box, pointing toward the orange door. Pretend to stumble or something when you place it and keep walking west on Tenth toward Washington Street. Walk slowly, like you're drugged or drunk or something."

"No problem there."

Sydney grinned, head down. "Please wear the gloves and tuck your hair into a hat. Don't be identifiable on any cameras and make sure the camera has no fingerprints. Same thing goes for the stakeout tonight. At nine P.M. sharp, you and Lily should be parked at the fire hydrant on Greenwich on the east side of the street, a few cars south of Tenth. Here, I've written everything down. It's a lot to remember. Any questions?"

"Just sit in the car with Lily?"

"Yes. Sit with the car off and wait for my directions on the walkie-talkie."

"Do I need to carry?"

"No. You'll just be following a car or two."

"Okay. Only problem is, uh, your sister."

"What about her?"

"I doubt she'll want to do this."

Forty-five

SYDNEY HAD AN unobstructed view of the front sidewalk, the orange door entrance, and the town house garage. No had one exited or entered since David had placed the camera at three A.M. *David aced it.*

Around eight that night, Sydney received a cryptic e-mail from Johnny.

> 2 plates = Cadillac STS & CTS/Fenly/Queens, 1 plate = Mercedes SL 550/Barrett/Upper East Side, 1 plate = Nissan Maxima/Petri/Yonkers.

The SUV plate's either stolen or altered. It's registered to a Nissan Maxima. The owner's name, Petri, is probably wrong too.

Nine P.M., she was in the West Village. The thick, humid air made it feel more like the New Orleans bayou than New York City. The sky was inky black, there was no breeze, and it was eerily silent. Sydney saw David dozing in the driver's seat of his beat-up green Ford. Lily lounged next to him, head back, eyes closed.

Sydney strolled past David's car, lobbing a burner cell phone through the open driver's-side window. "Wake up," she hissed without breaking stride. Then she sat on the west-side curb of Greenwich, a few cars south of Tenth Street. Sydney's handheld phone was synced to the camera outside the town house, projecting an open view of the street and the house's front and garage doors.

Lit by old-fashioned street lamps, the West Village was dimmer than most other neighborhoods in Manhattan. The warm breeze swirled up Tenth Street from the Hudson River as droplets of soft rain started to fall. Men walked hand in hand; colorful umbrellas popped open. A teenaged couple moved their dog and backpacks under a storefront awning. No movement from the orange door.

At 10:22, the rain poured down in torrents. David radioed Sydney.

"Yo, Syd, Lily's gettin' ants in her pants. She wants to book. She doesn't understand why she needs to be here with me."

"It's less suspicious if a couple is sitting in a car talking than a man alone. Tell her to suck it up," Sydney whispered into the walkie-talkie.

"Got it."

About twenty minutes later, Fenly's car pulled into the parking lot on Greenwich Street. A bolt of lightning zigzagged in the sky as he scurried across the street. A snap of thunder boomed. A navy-blue SUV swung around the corner. The garage door hummed, sliding up, then down. Sydney pushed a button on her soaked watch. *Will the timing be the same as last night?* The garage door reopened six minutes later. *Same.* The SUV pulled out and drove to the parking lot, taking a spot next to Fenly's car. It was the same driver as the night before, with the same bogus license plate. *Looks like Fenly's the front guy, the "legit" money launderer, and the SUV guy transports and trafficks.*

Sydney thought about sticking trackers on both vehicles right then but decided against it. If the parking lot had a camera, it was too risky. And if someone else was coming, it could blow her cover. Fourteen minutes elapsed and the garage door lifted. A silver BMW rounded the corner and drove in. The driver resembled the man in the Mercedes from the night before, perhaps a bit older. His black suit jacket offset his styled gray hair.

She radioed David. "I expect movement in about forty-five minutes. Be ready."

"Not for nothin', Syd. Are we just gonna sit here and do nothin' if somethin' is going on in that house?" David asked.

"Yup. Tonight we're fucking eating it. I don't know what this is yet, but whoever took Robbie is careful and organized, 'cause he's still missing. This organization may be big and lots of kids may be at risk."

"Your call, Syd."

Shit. This is like disaster triage, when you have to decide who lives and who dies.

Forty-seven minutes later, when the garage door lifted, the BMW pulled out.

"David. Silver BMW, traveling east on Tenth, follow from two cars behind," she said.

"On it."

A few minutes later, he called to report that the car had turned into a private garage in a town house on Gramercy Park. Sydney asked him to return.

David arrived on Greenwich just as the SUV driver exited the house, retrieved his vehicle, and drove back into the garage. The door closed; four minutes later, it reopened; the SUV pulled away.

"David, I've got the SUV. Take the Caddy when it moves," Sydney said into the walkie-talkie. "Slap a tracker under the rear bumper once the car stops for the night. Take the SIM card and batteries out of the phone, break them, and toss them. Then you're done. Just one more thing—please retrieve, smash, and trash the flower box camera sometime during the day tomorrow. Thanks, David. Thank Lily, too. Good job."

On Forty-Second Street, the SUV stopped at a light. The Broadway theaters had just let out for the evening, and the streets were teeming with cars from New Jersey and Philadelphia headed toward the Lincoln Tunnel. Crowds of fast-walking New Yorkers lined the sidewalks, navigating chaotic Times Square. Traffic was tight as Sydney drove up to the left tire well of the SUV, out of the side mirror's sightline. She stuck the tracker in the tire well. Hanging back about six cars, she followed it up the West Side Highway, to the Saw Mill, and onto the Taconic. Forty-eight miles north, the SUV exited right before Peekskill, by FDR Park. Sydney passed the SUV as it pulled into the park.

A half mile down a deserted, leafy, tree-lined street, Sydney stopped by the side of the road. She exchanged her dark blue helmet for a red one and added a long-sleeved leather jacket. She turned the bike around, waiting with the headlights off. When the tracker indicated that the SUV emerged from the park, she followed. Even from afar, she saw that its license plate had changed from New York to Connecticut.

The SUV reentered the Taconic Parkway northbound and traveled to I-82. Traffic was light, so Sydney kept her distance. Thirty-five miles later, the SUV turned off at the Greentree, Connecticut, exit. And so did Sydney. She sped up, passed the SUV, and pulled into an all-night gas station.

Her phone was vibrating; it read:

> Forest Hills. Name Fenly. David.

She texted Johnny. Monitoring the tracker, she trailed about a mile behind the SUV.

Blue Trees Way was a deadly quiet, newly paved country lane guarded by a canopy of trees that blocked the light from the stars and moon, rendering it pitch-black. The road cut through the forest, tucking each sprawling ranch home into a twenty- to twenty-five-acre land parcel. Although the tracker registered the location of the SUV, all Sydney could detect from the road was a windy driveway surrounded by trees and rows of thick, wide bushes.

When she Googled the street, a white-and-red-shingled ranch house with an attached garage and rambling backyard popped up.

Her burner phone vibrated.

>Plate = Ford Explorer/Anderson/Greentree. J

Forty-Six

"Ma," Sydney said as she entered her mother's bedroom.

"What, what time is it?" she asked.

"It's late, but I have to give you something," Sydney said.

"I mean, really Sydney, wait 'til tomorrow!"

"No. It can't wait. Here," she said quietly, trying not to awaken Lily. She walked over to her mother's bed, handing her an envelope with ten packets of $100 bills, her will, her apartment deed, and the names of her lawyer and accountant.

"Put this away someplace safe and make sure Lily doesn't ever find it."

"What are you giving me?"

"Some important information plus cash. In case something happens. It's for you and Lily. It'll take care of you for a couple of years. And, Ma, don't use it if you don't need to. Like, if I'm still around. Like to gamble."

"What do you mean, 'in case something happens'?"

"Think about taking Lily to the relatives in Canada for a while. It might help clear her head. New atmosphere, new people."

"What do you mean 'in case something happens,' Sydney?"

"I have to go, Ma. I'll speak to you later."

"Sydney!" she hissed. "You're not going to get involved with finding that boy, are you? It's not your problem, Sydney. Big money means big risk. This isn't a game. It's serious and dangerous."

"Bye, Ma." She turned to leave.

"Understand something, Sydney. It may go way up high. People are a lot dirtier than you can imagine. Leave it alone."

Sydney was in the hallway that led out of the room. Her back faced her mother.

"Sydney!" Her mom pitter-pattered over to her. "I know you never give up. I get it. Ever since you were a little girl and sparred with your father, you would never quit and he would never quit. Even when it was clear that you were losing, even that time when your fingers were broken, you never quit."

"But by ten, I was beating him, Ma."

"Then finish it, Sydney. No loose ends."

Forty-Seven

J, GO TO Blue Trees Way, pass the ranch. 2.2 miles east, there's a wooded outlet. Didn't see any cameras. Launch electric drone from there. Rock at 1.

Sydney pressed send at six A.M.

Late morning, she eased onto the Taconic entrance ramp continuing at a moderate pace onto the blue-black, thick-tree-lined, vacant parkway. A cool breeze seeped underneath her helmet as she took the undulating curves with a gentle brake and rapid acceleration. On the occasional straightaways, she picked up speed zipping north.

She was making great time until she rounded a bend and approximately five hundred feet ahead the traffic was at a complete standstill. She squeezed the hand brake and tapped the foot brake. The front brake collapsed inward with no deceleration, and the foot brake plunged downward in a spongy but unreactive fashion. She pumped the foot brake again. Nothing. *What the...*

She downshifted—fifth gear, fourth, third; the gears ground. The gap was closing fast, two hundred feet...one hundred feet, still no traffic movement. With less than twenty-five feet left before smashing into the cars, Sydney swerved to the right, bouncing over the curb and onto the grass. She dragged the soles of her cowboy boots on the ground to create resistance, ripping the turf apart. Shifting to second, then first, the bike bolted toward the tree line. Ten feet out, she shot her left leg over the seat, cranked the handlebars hard to the left, and slid the bike onto its side. She rode the mass of metal right up to the forest edge, then rolled off, sinking hard into the soft grass.

The slide was nothing new for her. She'd done it countless times before with Johnny when they jumped dirt bikes. But those bikes had engine protectors; the red Ducati looked like a bloodied beached whale.

"HEY, ARE YOU OKAY? SOMEONE CALL NINE-ONE-ONE!" called out a driver as others ran toward her.

"I'M FINE. NO NEED FOR NINE-ONE-ONE!" she shouted back. She wanted to investigate but waited.

She approached the broken mess and examined the front brake cable and noticed a paper-thin cut through the plastic protective covering; frayed metal ends protruded. No brake fluid was present in the container.

Thirty minutes later, a tow truck pulled up. She asked the driver to take her to a motorcycle repair shop in downtown Manhattan, happy that it fell within the one-hundred-mile free towing radius her AAA gold card allowed. For the next forty minutes, she rode in the truck's cab next to Billy, a quiet man with long auburn hair and short, greasy fingernails. Every couple of miles Billy perked up asking her a question or two about the bike. Talking distracted her from thinking about its poor condition, as it lay tethered to the truck's flatbed.

She texted Johnny.

Delayed.

Around one, they were in front of the Red Hot Ducati Shop. As Billy jumped down from the driver's seat, Vinny, the owner and chief mechanic, walked out and pointed to a spot.

"Hey, Sydney. What the *hell*?" he asked.

"Take a look, Vinny. Brake trouble."

He walked to the bike, bending slightly to inspect the brakes, then stood up. "Listen Sydney, I just inspected your bike in May. Someone messed with this. There's a pinhole cut in your brake fluid containers, and the cables are frayed. You need to report it. It amazes me that you're alive, kiddo. You must have mad skills."

"No police. It'll be a pain, and they won't find anyone. How about lending me a bike while you fix it? If I break it, you know I'll buy it."

"No problem. This will take at least a week to fix. Which bike do you want? Pick."

She pointed to a black older-model Ducati. "That one would be great, Vinny. Thanks a ton."

"Go across the street and grab a coffee; the paperwork will take at least twenty minutes."

Two men wearing light blue shirts with PAUL'S PLUMBING stenciled on the back in navy thread sat at the counter of this dingy diner consuming stacks of pancakes and chunks of Canadian ham. Sydney took a seat in a burgundy faux-leather booth by the window. She wanted the "lumberjack"—three eggs, four pancakes, bacon, sausage, and burned French fries—but the task ahead made her reconsider. Instead, she ordered three hard-boiled eggs, fruit salad, and a freshly baked corn muffin.

By her third cup of stale coffee, she noticed Vinnie waving her back. She mounted the bike and he said, "Be careful, Sydney. This is no joke."

"José, hi, it's Sydney Chang in 20P. My motorcycle broke this morning, and I'd like to review some video from out front."

The basement of her apartment complex housed a sterile room with a desk, a chair, and an old Dell computer. The sign on the door read BUILDING MANAGER. When Sydney knocked, José, a balding, stocky middle-aged man, waved her in. "What kind of bike do you have, Doctor?"

"A red Ducati."

He motioned her over. "I see your bike all the time. Help yourself while I go check on the water heater."

As she fast-forwarded through the video, she spotted her bike. No one near it; she kept the feed flying. Then she saw someone. She stopped, rewound, and slowed it down. The video was time stamped four A.M. and dated this morning. A slim, athletically built, approximately six-foot-tall man in a black cap stood next to it, then crouched. About four minutes later he popped up, looked around, and sauntered away.

Forty-Eight

DRONE FEED IMAGES flashed onto the overhead screens as Sydney rushed into Johnny's cellar. She handed him a flash drive.

"Someone took out the brakes on my bike," she said.

"Shit," he said.

"I have a loaner. Please put the flash drive up on one screen, the drone feed in the middle, and the news feed of the unidentified boy and woman on the other," she said.

"The bike sabotage is a problem, Syd." He loaded the footage. "Could it be someone else, like from Lily's world?"

"Unfortunately, yes. But let's focus on the blond woman and the kid."

"You think it's someone from inside the hospital?" he asked as he corrected the video resolution.

"Could be, but Jimmy said everyone was vetted."

"Who's Jimmy?"

"Head of hospital security. I've known him for years since he started as a security guard."

The screen was filled with a verdant backyard blanketed with grass and trees, plus two rectangular concrete areas. One was a cutout with a standard-sized basketball hoop. The other, larger section held a picnic table with chairs and a high-end grill. Two battered Dunkin' Donuts boxes, paper plates, and milk cartons covered the table. Johnny and Sydney stared at a woman who looked to be in her early forties, with dark hair, a wide forehead, and a narrow nose.

They counted three boys, two blonds, one dark-haired, and one girl, also dark-haired. The straw-colored blond with a small, straight, nose and large blue eyes roamed aimlessly. The white-blond boy sat in the distance by a tree. The brown-haired and angelic-looking boy sat quietly on the basketball court looking up at the sky. Sydney judged their ages to be between seven and eleven. The girl, a black, curly-haired beauty with sea-green eyes, honey-beige skin, and a turned-up nose, probably five or six years old, sat at the table, expressionless, with folded hands.

Staring at the footage, Sydney asked, "Is it possible we've invented a whole scenario, and this is just a family with a lot of kids? But they don't look like any of the adults, and they don't look like siblings; maybe they're adopted?"

"The SUV plate is registered to Anderson at this address. I looked up the Greentree town school registry. It lists five kids, and they're registered as homeschooled. So we're not seeing them all," Johnny said.

Connecting to the face-match program at missingkids.com, Johnny downloaded shots of each kid. Next he performed an open search in New York and Connecticut that fielded hundreds of photos of missing children—endangered and runaways. Zero hits.

"Don't you think these kids are unusually quiet for their age?" Sydney asked.

"I guess."

"They don't play. Or run around. They just sit," Sydney said.

"Well, if you looked at a video of us at that age, we were the same; we sat just like them."

"No, only you did."

"Oh yeah. You ran around like crazy," he said.

"Let's run through our options."

"If we anonymously call the FBI and report that we saw the 'boy' from the news report, do you think they'll have the local cops go to the house and question them?" Johnny asked.

"Most likely. They get a lot of anonymous messages, and these guys are used to following the chain of command. But if the Andersons are what we think they are, it will be disastrous for Robbie, especially if there's a dirt problem with the local cops," she said.

"I agree. What if we stake out the property and sneak in? Once we locate Robbie, we can take him. But can we leave the other kids behind?" he asked.

"No. Sneaking in will take more surveillance and time. And the longer they have Robbie, the more danger he's in. If I'm spotted, the viciousness of the attack and the collateral damage will be higher. Tonight's the best option. We'll have to get all the kids out, Robbie or no Robbie. But if we're wrong, *we'll* be the kidnappers. We'll drop the kids off near a police station, but not the local one. Did you call your sister?"

"Yeah, Chrissy's coming," he said.

Johnny whipped out a new phone, inserted the battery and SIM card. They inputted contacts and e-mail addresses: Detective Thomas and his precinct, the local Connecticut police, and the FBI. They included the news media: the *New York Times*, the *Post*, the *Daily News*, CNN, BBC, CNC (Chinese international news), and SKY News. They added the ACLU, human trafficking NGOs, PolarisProject.org, the National Center for Missing and Exploited Children, the Blue Heart Campaign, and the National Human Trafficking Resource Center (NHTRC).

Another kid appeared on the video as he exited the house onto the patio. He was older than the rest and scruffy, maybe seventeen. He, too, was handsome, but his eyes were hollowed. Dark rings circled them. Perhaps he was an older brother. In a zombielike state, he sat down at the table.

"Go back and freeze-frame the feed on the boy by the tree, Johnny. Enlarge it," Sydney said, leaning toward the screen. "Something about him is familiar. Run the hospital news clip. I want to see them side by side. Look at the way he gnaws on his thumb knuckle." They zoomed in on the enlarged shot of the blond woman and boy in the hospital. "He looks different. But same knuckle, same gnaw."

The dark-haired woman waved her hand, signaling the kids inside. Like robots, they marched in. The boy by the tree didn't budge. She approached him, and he scooted his rear around the tree with his back facing her.

"With cosmetic alteration and a blond wig, like Lily said, we may be looking at the woman from the hospital; she's the same height and build," Sydney said and stood. Sydney and Johnny watched her call out to the boy.

No response and no movement from him. A midforties-ish male appeared in the back door frame. He was unshaven, unkempt, and supersized. If they had a smell feature on the camera, he'd surely reek. He yelled out toward the boy.

"He doesn't look like the guy who messed up my bike."

The kid just sat chewing. The woman shot a look at the man, who grimaced. She strode over to the boy, grabbed his hand out of his mouth, and tugged. The boy rose, hung his head, and stuck the knuckle back in.

"It's him. That's the boy from the hospital," said Sydney.

Forty-Nine

"**T**OUGH TIMES, HUH?" Chrissy said as she swung her tanned, lean leg off of her white motorcycle in front of Johnny's house.

"Yeah. Thanks for helping out. I appreciate it," Sydney said as the dusky evening air clung like cheap drugstore lotion on her cheeks.

Chrissy wore a yellow sundress tucked between her legs, a jean jacket, beige espadrilles, and a white full-faced helmet. Her wavy golden hair cascaded down her back. Sydney smiled.

"Glad to. How's Lily and Mom?" Chrissy asked.

"Mom's good, Lily, not so much."

"Shame, such a smart girl," Chrissy said.

A full head taller than Johnny, Chrissy had green eyes that sparkled like her mother's. They were rimmed with smudged onyx liner and painted with iridescent turquoise shadow. A few crinkled, dry mascara droppings were stuck on the midnight-blue-tinged flesh underneath her bottom lids, but she still had those rosy, wide cheekbones and the gleaming smile. With a cinched waist and sizable chest, she rocked a hot body. She'd always been a sharp kid; she knew how to handle herself.

Sydney motioned Chrissy to follow, and in Johnny's living room, she handed her clothes.

"Please change into these," Sydney said.

Chrissy stripped down, then slipped on Sydney's light-colored, blousy pants and loose, long-sleeved shirt, buttoning it up to her collarbone. She tied a paper-thin cotton scarf around her neck to ensure that every inch of her tanned skin was covered. She slid on Sydney's cropped black leather jacket and maneuvered her mane into a tight bun. Pulling Sydney's navy helmet onto her head and snapping shut the black-out shield, she camouflaged her face. Men's camel-colored leather gloves and a pair of dark cowboy boots completed her transformation.

Chrissy's job was to make sure the cameras, especially the tollbooth ones far away from the action site, recorded her as Sydney. Chrissy had no problem mimicking Sydney's aggressive riding style; she knew that well.

"Johnny briefed you?" Sydney asked.

"He did; I've got the routes and timing memorized. He's gonna put my bike and clothes at the old swimming pond, and I'll switch out when he calls. Heeeeyy, Johnny," Chrissy said as she passed him on her way out the front door. "I got a gift for ya, honey." She handed him her dress, jean jacket, espadrilles, and helmet. He nodded.

Sydney stood by the living room window watching Chrissy drive away on the Red Hot Ducati Shop's loaner bike.

"I'm going to change. I'll meet you at the site at nine fifteen sharp," Sydney said.

Johnny shot one thumb up and headed outside to modify the license plate on his bike.

To create a bit of subterfuge, Sydney rode Johnny's dirt bike north on and around local highways for twelve miles. Then she switched, heading south down a different route. By the time she approached the house on Blue Trees Way, it was dark. A hint of pine and moist loam filled her nostrils. She welcomed the coolness as she dismounted, attached her helmet to the handlebars, and turned off the engine. She checked her compass. With the aid of the moon's illumination, she pushed the bike into the shadowy woods. An occasional cicada chirp and insect chatter rang out amidst the snaps and crackles of the breaking branches as she rolled over the dry underbrush. Two hundred yards and five minutes later, a sliver of artificial light pierced the darkness. She paused, looking around. When she spotted a cluster of tightly grouped pine trees, she forcibly maneuvered the bike out of sight into the narrow space between them and quietly continued toward the brightness. When the house was in full focus, she checked her compass and retraced her path out past the bike.

Masked by a tree's shadow on an empty road at the forest's edge, she waited for Johnny. At nine fifteen P.M., he pulled up in a navy commercial E-series Ford van that he'd "borrowed" earlier in the day. With altered license plates, a reinforced front bumper, disabled airbags, and a "kill switch"–rigged engine, he inched toward Sydney. She opened the creaky rear door and climbed in. He grinned. Unrecognizable in a fitted blond wig; discolored, slightly protruding false teeth; ivory-colored foundation; hazel contact lenses; and black gloves, she nodded. In the back of the van, she slipped into a bulletproof vest outfitted with a body camera. With a long-sleeved dark shirt buttoned up to her neck, she called out, "Ready."

Johnny stopped by the side of the road. He jumped out of the driver's seat and headed to the back of the van as she climbed into the front. Sydney maneuvered the old van around the woods on the quiet back roads. As she glanced into the rearview mirror, their eyes met briefly. His were now brown; he had a black shaggy mustache, and his hair was hidden beneath a baseball cap.

"Finish it, Syd. Jail time will be forever if you're caught, finished or not. I hope you find him."

Fifty

STUFFED INTO A forest clearing the size of a tight one-car garage, Sydney and Johnny waited in the pitch black on a side street about a mile south of Blue Trees Way. Johnny monitored the tracking device of the Anderson SUV on his phone.

"They just exited off the highway. I expect them to pass in six to seven minutes," he said.

"Okay," she replied and grabbed the steering wheel with two hands.

Minutes later, "Approaching," he said.

As the backlights of the SUV disappeared, Sydney floored the gas, bolting out of the bushes. She caught up to the SUV and rear-ended it. Swerving to the right, the SUV half spun and came to an abrupt stop.

The driver from the other night, the same man from the West Village town house, stepped out, looking shaken. Sydney approached him.

"What the fuck?" he said to her.

"So sorry. I guess I was going too fast," she said as she stood next to him. "I'm Devin. I have my insurance card here. You are?"

"Tim."

He bent down to examine the damage and—*zzzzzzzz*—Sydney Tasered his neck. He fell. She whipped out a needle and injected a ketamine-midazolam mixture. Johnny carried him to their van as Sydney climbed into the SUV. A young boy, maybe nine, sat motionless with headlight eyes.

"I'm not going to hurt you. I'm here to help you. I'm going to put you to sleep for a few minutes, and when you wake up, you'll be back with the other kids, okay?" Sydney said.

He nodded slowly.

Sydney injected him then gently tied his arms and feet. She couldn't chance him waking up and running around. She carried the boy into their van as Johnny finished hog-tying the SUV man; his ID read Timothy Anderson. Exiting, Johnny handed Sydney a pocket-sized electronic button.

"Here's the panic button," he said.

"Again, one press, call nine-one-one, give them the address and info about the other locations, and leave. No discussion, just leave. If I hit it twice, I need your help; come into the house. Text Chrissy now to switch bikes and start heading over here," Sydney said.

After ripping the tracker off of the SUV, Johnny drove it, lights off, to the side of the Anderson's driveway. He parked it out of sight. When he hopped back into their van, he sat in the back with the new passengers. Sydney turned onto the Andersons' property.

The moment the van's front tires crunched onto the gravel of the property's driveway, Sydney hit the rig button. Smoke billowed out from under the hood. The vehicle jerked, ground, and spewed its way down the circular path, rattling to a stop a few feet from the entrance of the house. Sydney stepped out, grabbed her Taser off of the passenger seat, and walked toward the wooden front door. She waited with the weapon hidden behind her hip, pressed flush against her body. Light from the front room streamed out of the four bay windows. She heard a television in the distance. She knocked. No response. The van started hissing.

"Hello! Hello! Just had a car accident with a guy named Tim. He said he lives here, and I should come get you. Hello! There's a child involved. Hello!"

Click. The lock turned. The door opened. One step forward and—*zzzzzz*—she stunned the oversized man in the neck; he dropped to one knee. She grabbed the expandable metal baton taped to the back of her right lower leg, flicked it open, and slammed it across his face. Down. *Whack!* She took out his knees. Stepping on the back of his arm, right above the elbow, she yanked his lower arm back. *Snap!* Plastic cuffs joined his hands and ankles behind his back. She ripped off a sheet of precut duct tape from under her jacket sleeve and slapped it onto his mouth. She rolled a thin black stocking mask down over her face and secured her wig up and into the back of it.

From the feed, she knew at least one more adult, one teen, and four kids were in the house. Moving stealthily over the pristine oak floors in the living room, she checked under the two brown leather couches. A flat-screen television and a square glass table rounded out the rest of the furniture. The room was clear.

She passed through the dining area clearing the space under a country-style table, then looked into the kitchen. Three modern windows overlooked the backyard and tangled woods. A rectangular white Formica table, two long white counters, and several wooden chairs were scattered about. Off the kitchen was a bathroom, empty. She removed a shred of paper from her jacket pocket, placed it in the bathroom door hinge, and closed the door. If it opened or closed, she would know. Moving toward a foyer, she saw it. A camera affixed to the ceiling aiming at a simple, plain door with a dead-bolt lock—unlocked. She slid the bolt to the locked position. She rounded the corner and entered the master bedroom. Peeking under the bed, into the closet, and into the master bathroom, she came up empty.

Next bedroom. She tiptoed to the door, gently turning the knob. She pushed the door completely open, and rays of ambient light from the living room broke through the shadowy darkness. She saw the rumpled bedsheets and felt a breeze as a table lamp flew past her head, smashing against the wall. A body barreled toward her, carrying a raised bat. A swift kick to the chest and a back fist to the head, and he fell. The bat clattered to the floor. She straddled and pinned the groaning, wiggling form. "Where's the boy they took from the hospital?" she asked.

"Fuck you!" Her hand pressed a piece of duct tape onto the mouth of the teenage boy from the video. Removing a syringe from a cigar-sized metal case, she injected him. His body went limp. After a quick hog-tie, Sydney searched the rest of the main floor. Empty. Total time: five minutes, thirty-five seconds.

In the foyer, Sydney whipped the metal baton across the lens of the ceiling camera, shattering it. Positioned in front of the door adjacent to the kitchen, she slid the dead bolt back, switched off the overhead light, and cracked the door. Crouching, Sydney entered the dimly lit staircase. Baton in hand, she removed a *shuriken*, a throwing star, from her pants pocket, and silently descended. The stairway opened into a landing: one room directly across from it and another longer room to the right with a floor-to-ceiling, closed accordion divider. A soft yellow light seeped out from under the two-inch gap between the white vinyl floor tiles and the divider's bottom edge.

It was still when she placed her boot on the second-to-last step. A split second later, a muzzle flashed. She threw the *shuriken* at the light. In the illuminated millisecond, Sydney spotted someone recessed back in the dark room. *Pop!* Something slammed into Sydney's right side. A woman screamed. Sydney collapsed backward, striking her right side on a step. She lay sprawled on the stairs with the air knocked out of her. Every inhalation radiated pain from armpit to armpit. The bulletproof jacket had worked. It had prevented the penetration of the bullet, but the impact was shocking, and falling on the step hadn't helped.

Sydney heard short, raspy breaths. Her unblinking eyes were slits. Through the sliver-like openings, she watched the woman close in. Bent over with an outstretched shaking arm, pistol pointed at Sydney's head, *shuriken* lodged into her opposite shoulder, her grip tightened. Rolling toward her, Sydney kicked her leg straight up into the woman's arm. It repositioned the gun. *Bang!* The bullet hit the ceiling; the shooter stumbled back. Dripping with sweat and panting, Sydney swung the metal baton into the woman's left hand, and the gun clanked to the floor. She swiped her knee. *Crack!* The woman shrieked, collapsing. Elbows next. The shrieking escalated. Sydney tore a piece of tape off of her jacket and held it in her hand.

"Where's the boy you took from the hospital?" she puffed in a deep, muffled voice as she hovered over the woman's prostrate body.

"What boy?" she whimpered.

Shit, are they actually just a normal family? Sydney smacked tape on the moaner's mouth and bound her arms and legs together.

With shallow breaths, Sydney reached down and picked up the gun. She bent from the waist, opened her mouth wide, and gasped for air. Sydney shuffled into the nearby room. Her right rib cage rattled.

Sydney flicked the light on in the windowless room. It had a standard desk, computer, chair, and a narrow green couch.

Stacks of cash lined the table in high neat piles. From a quick glance, it looked like thousands. The computer screen showed a graph filled with numbers and names. Behind the desk, a wall safe's door was ajar. *Later.*

Moving into the other room, she pulled on the partition handle. Locked. She sliced a human sized X into the accordion partition and stepped through. In the far corner of the poorly lit room, huddled together and cowering, a bunch of kids stared. As Sydney approached, their heads tilted downward, their shoulders pointed up, and their arms hung slackly against their sides. They braced themselves like a bunch of puppies recoiling from an abusive owner. Every so often their eyes flicked up, sneaking peeks at the figure in the black stocking face mask.

She counted seven children—four boys, three girls. No Robbie.

Fifty-One

"You have to leave here now. I'm going to help you, not hurt you. Come with me," Sydney said to the children.

"We're not going with you," one kid immediately mumbled.

"Okay. Okay," she whispered in a low husky grunt. "But I have a question. Anyone see this boy?" Her arm extended with Robbie's photo. She turned to the outspoken, older kid—the boy from the video, the knuckle biter. As Sydney moved closer, the children pressed their backs into the wall.

The children watched her, expressionless.

"Anyone know him?"

They shook their heads slowly.

Supporting her spine against the wall, Sydney looked directly into the eyes of the blond boy. "You've seen him. Is he anywhere on the property?" she panted.

"No," he muttered, turning his head to the left.

"Are these all of the kids in the house?" she asked.

They silently stared at her.

"Okay, I know you don't want to, but you have to leave here. I'm going to give you two choices. Come with me. Or hide in the woods until the police come to help you. Please put on your shoes."

Sydney stepped back through the partition's X. She tensed her midsection and dragged the woman's body into the office. Stepping on her shattered knee, Sydney asked, "Where's the boy from the hospital?" as she ripped the tape off of her mouth. The woman groaned, lips pressed together. The tape was slapped back on. *I should pull the* shuriken *from her shoulder. No. She'll bleed out.*

Sydney swept the desktop's and safe's contents—flash drives, DVDs, cell phone, and cash—into a rolled-up bag. She took one more look into the safe. That's when she saw it, all the way in the back, almost hidden: a panic button. *Gotta get these kids out now.* She placed the gun inside and locked the safe.

Stepping over the woman, Sydney said, "You'll get your stuff back when I get the boy you stole from hospital," as she pulled the door shut.

Sydney popped her head back through the opening. "Let's go, guys."

The blond boy took a few steps toward Sydney. "Where's Joyce?" he asked with a touch of bravado, then stepped back, tripping on one of the seated children, who let out a whimper. He slouched his shoulders, folded his arms in front of his chest, and dropped back even more.

"Joyce can't help you. Someone dangerous is coming. You guys need to leave—now," she said softly, pausing to catch her breath.

"Is Joyce okay?" he asked in a shaky voice.

"Yes. Did you all decide what you want to do?"

"Woods."

Sydney led. The blond boy followed her tentatively. The little ones were next, and the eldest girl took up the rear. Sydney plodded up the steps, walked through the kitchen, and leaned against the back door keeping it open as the kids passed through. When the last one cleared, she said authoritatively, "Run! Go far into the woods. Hide and be quiet. Don't come out until you see big lights, cameras, and police. Do. Not. Come. Out."

"Charlie is missing. He was with Tim. Where is he?" the blond boy said, turning around.

"He's coming."

When they entered the woods and were no longer visible, Sydney scrambled through the house and exited the front door. She knocked on the hood of the van. Johnny opened the door.

"Did you find Robbie?"

"No. A panic button was pushed. Trouble's coming, maybe Fenly. Monitor his tracker. The kids chose the woods. Bring Tim into the house; I'll take the boy. Then go," she said. She handed him the bag, bent over, and exhaled. "I'm staying. I need to see who's coming. I took their stuff; it might keep Robbie alive. Check the SIM card on the phone. Give me the tracker from the SUV. I may need it. Don't notify the authorities until I press the electronic button once."

She untied the boy who was groggy but awake. "Come with me; your friends are asking for you, Charlie," she said. Sydney led him into the woods and called out, "Charlie's here, come get him." The blond boy sprinted out from behind a tree.

Her phone vibrated.

Fenly's car coming. Just exited parkway.

Behind a maple tree on the left side of the woods, she inhaled a deeper, stronger breath. Unbuttoning her overshirt, she exposed the body cam lens and hit video. She heard the crunch of car tires on gravel. The engine clicked off. Two doors creaked open but closed with barely a sound. Footfalls scrunched on the pebbles. The surrounding woods were motionless—no leaves rustled, no animals moved, only an occasional bird chirped. No new lights turned on in the house, no voices, no noise, nothing filtered out. Until, from inside the house, *Pfut! Pfut!* The woods exploded with a cacophony of chirping, hooting, and the pitter-patter of animal feet on the run. *Gunshots.*

Fifty-Two

THE KITCHEN DOOR burst open. Two men rushed into the backyard. Both carried large metal containers. The stout one was Fenly. The other man, with a dark baseball cap pulled low on his forehead, strode across the lawn toward the opposite side of the woods from Sydney. He wore khakis and a long-sleeved white shirt, but as he proceeded deeper into the woods, Sydney lost sight of him. She depended on sound alone, but with the clanking of Fenly's metal container, she struggled to hear his footsteps. Suddenly, about fifty yards back and seventy yards to her right, a faint creak and a pale light shone into the woods.

What's that from? Sydney controlled her shallow breathing. She crept forward slowly, acutely aware of the dry forest floor crumpling under her boots. Fenly drenched the outside border of the house with liquid. Sydney was about twenty yards from the underground light when the man emerged from the hole dragging a large duffel bag. Then she smelled it: the pungent scent of gasoline. The man lit a match. She sprinted toward him. He dropped it down the hole. One swift fan of the trapdoor, a hissing sound, loud crackling noises, and *BOOM!* A violent flash of fire exploded as flames shot out and licked the opened hatch. He lifted the duffel bag and ran toward the house. Sydney dashed toward the cellar and looked over the edge. Blue-white flames exploded into the air as Sydney spotted a small white sneaker roasting. Raw, red-hot fury rose from deep within her gut; her nostrils flared, her eyes narrowed, and the saliva in her mouth evaporated.

"Give me your car keys," he yelled to Fenly. The voice was oddly familiar, but she couldn't place it. "Light it."

"I'll start inside," Fenly replied as he handed him the keys.

Fenly opened the kitchen door as the other man reached into the back of his waistband. A glint of light reflected off of the gun in his hand. *Pfut! Pfut!* She saw two bright flashes and heard a muffled thump. Fenly was down. The man scurried into the house. Sydney cut through the front of the woods like a famished lion pursuing a deer. She hit the electronic button once. Blue flames danced behind the kitchen windows, and the glass shattered as blazes tore through the house with a scorching roar.

The man was a few feet from the car when—*slash*. With a metal baton, she ripped the side of his face. He fell and the bag slid out from under his arm. Blood gushed from his right cheek and dripped onto the gravel. His cap tumbled off. Bob Inger's bloodied face looked up at her.

Winded, Sydney stood over him, inhaling quick, tiny puffs. Inger's eyelids fluttered. Out of the corner of her eye, she thought she saw the dropped bag move. She glanced at it and—*click*. His trigger lock was off. Light glinted off of the semiautomatic pistol in his hand. *Pfut!* It grazed her right side. Lunging forward, she grabbed the pistol barrel and pushed it back with force. Inger pulled the trigger again. The weapon didn't fire. Sydney knew it wouldn't. She pushed the barrel release and in one smooth motion slid it off as she back fisted him in the face. Slamming the barrel into his collarbone, she just missed her intended target—his neck. He groaned and squirmed, pushing her off of his shoulder and smashing his head into her chest. She fell back.

Inger scrambled to his feet, touched his face, and scowled. He glanced at the black-clad masked figure, then dashed over to the bag and ran it to the car. Sydney struggled to stand. Racked with pain, she slowly rose. Inger popped the trunk of Fenly's car, dumping the bag in. Gravel spit back, hitting her pant legs as she reached the trunk. Inger tore out of the driveway. Sirens wailed in the distance.

Billows of smoke overwhelmed the evening sky swallowing it whole. The heat was intense. Hobbling back into the woods, she texted Johnny.

> Follow Fenly's car. Inger driving. Robbie in trunk?

She continued toward her bike when she heard something run past her. It was the blond kid dashing toward the house. *What the hell is he doing?* "STOP! Don't go near the house," she called out. He darted into the backyard, heading for the kitchen door. With baby breaths, she sprinted, her right arm plastered against her sliding ribs. She caught up just as he stepped through the open door. Flames burst out as she grabbed his shirt, whipping him onto the ground. On the grass, she smothered his engulfed shirtsleeve. Sirens blared.

"Stevie! Stevie's in there," the boy cried.

"I know. It's awful. I'm sorry," she said. The boy lay on the ground weeping, calling out Stevie's name. She heard car doors slam and feet scraping against the gravel. Sydney stood as quickly as she could and half jogged, half ran back into the woods.

"I got a kid here on the lawn. Just saw movement in the trees. Someone's out there. Go!" a male voice bellowed.

Bent over, she ran deeper into the forest glancing over her shoulder. She heard feet pounding through the underbrush...

fifty yards, thirty yards... She scurried through the brush and saw one hidden child.

"Go. Help is here. Go to the house," Sydney said. The kid stood frozen. She saw another one. "Help's here. Go. Run." Slowly, one moved, then a few others started running out from behind trees, and soon they all raced toward the house.

Grunting, she pulled Johnny's bike out of the tree cluster and pushed it onto the narrow path she'd forged earlier. When she cleared the woods, she draped herself onto the tank, flipped the bike on, and peeled out.

She traveled on back roads. At the first sign of a quiet, deserted place, about ten minutes later, she pulled over and texted Johnny.

> Send me tracking feed on Fenly's car. Let's all converge.

Sydney received the tracker feed. Light-headed, she sucked air puffs through her pursed lips and sped off. *Breathe. Focus. Do.*

Seeing his blip on her screen, no diagonal path to intercept him existed. The only way to catch him was to outrun him; he was only about eight miles ahead of her. *He's not speeding. Of course—he doesn't want to be pulled over.* About fifteen minutes later, she flew past him. Monitoring the car tracker, Sydney waited in the wooded shadows of the road's shoulder about a mile ahead. When his car was about a tenth of a mile, three curves, away, she rode the bike into the middle of the two-lane street and laid it on its side; lights on. He rounded the corner and abruptly slowed down, then swerved. *Perfect.* She stepped onto the road. His headlights spotlighted her. With the sawed-off shotgun braced against her right hip, she fired. She staggered slightly from its kickback. The front grille took a direct hit. The hood blew up, the engine hissed, and the car rolled onto the shallow grassy shoulder. Through a cloud of smoke, the front door swung open. Inger jumped out and ran into the woods.

Bent to her right side, she rushed to the car and pressed the trunk release button. She dragged the duffel bag out and onto the ground. Her heart pounded as she reached for the zipper. It was Robbie.

Fifty-Three

HIS EYES WERE closed; his left eye, swollen shut. His black-and-blue jaw was slack. His breathing was shallow. Sydney checked Robbie's pulse; it was strong. She checked his pupils; they were equal but contracted into pinpoints. She exhaled and nodded. On her knees, she dragged his sleeping body in the duffel bag onto the grass.

Johnny pulled up in the van just as Sydney reached Fenly's car and ripped the tracker out of the right rear tire well.

"Got him!" she said.

"Amazing! How's he doing?" Johnny said as he righted his bike and moved it out of the street.

"A bit banged up, but sleeping." Sydney reholstered the shotgun.

Two minutes later, Chrissy, dressed back in her own garb, rolled up on her own bike.

"Did you get the boy?" Chrissy asked.

"He's right there," Sydney said, smiling. "Hey, Chris. Johnny and I have to take off. Please call nine-one-one to report this and tell them a child is involved."

"You look like roadkill, Syd," said Chrissy.

"Yeah, you look too broken to ride. I'll take my bike, and you drive the van," Johnny said.

"Please don't leave Robbie until he's in an ambulance. Thank you both so much."

ABOUT TWENTY-FIVE MILES later, Sydney flipped on the van's hazard lights and motioned for Johnny to pull off the road.

fifty-four

"AN'T BREATHE," SHE said as he pulled up to the van's open window. "Open the bike bag."

She cleared the ink cartridge from a pen's cylinder. She handed it to Johnny.

"Plastic glove, cut off finger, make small slit in tip. Tape to pen cylinder; it'll act as one-way valve. Knife."

"Sydney?" Johnny stood over her.

She positioned the knife's point in the space above the top of her right rib, at T-4, just lateral to her breast. "Push it," she whispered. "Do it."

He hesitated, then placed his fingers on top of hers and pushed the knife into her chest. Sydney bit on her shirt. Through gritted teeth she said, "Twist."

Johnny turned it slightly, then slipped the cylinder in. Gas exited into the night air. Her respiratory rate decreased from over thirty panting breaths per minute to a more relaxed twenty. Her face calmed, and she took a deeper, yet still aching breath.

"Tape cylinder to my chest. Cut a hole in my shirt. It's just a tension pneumo."

"It was more fun when we just built go-karts and ate PBJs, right?" he said, his face ashen.

fifty-five

"OH, MAN, SYDNEY, you look like hell," Johnny said as Sydney woke up on his couch.

"I don't feel as bad as I look."

"I think we should go to the hospital now. You've done enough. Robbie's home."

"Let's just run through the drives from the house." Sydney tried to sit up, grimaced, and lay back. "What happened with the vehicles?"

"No worries. Everything's finished," he said as he plugged a flash drive into his laptop. The image of a middle-aged man fondling a young boy's genitals popped up onto the screen. "Look at this shit," Johnny said.

"Fast-forward," Sydney said as each frame depicted one depraved act after another. "Focus on the men's faces."

Three flash drives and two DVDs later, Sydney said, "Slow down; that's Inger."

"This is some gross shit. And some of them are major players, Syd."

"Yeah, I noticed. Please make twenty untraceable copies of Inger's segment and send copies of everything, including the body cam footage, to everyone on our list."

"I already made copies. Here's one for you. Chrissy and I will take care of the distribution. Tonight I'll get the police copies out, and in two days, I'll send out the media ones. I'll keep the originals. Give me five minutes, and I'll have those Inger copies ready. What about the cash?" said Johnny.

"Keep the cash. It's for the kids."

Fifty-Six

Using the hospital walls as support, she inched down the hallways until she reached the operating room's employee time clock. The area was unmonitored by cameras. With no one around, she tacked a clear plastic baggie containing several flash drives onto the wall right next to the clock. The label read: TAKE ONE AND WATCH NOW.

She was losing steam. Her next stop was the employee lunchroom, also empty. With gloved hands, she dumped a few flash drives with WATCH NOW Post-its affixed to them onto the main table.

Sydney shuffled back to her office. Her voice-mail light was blinking red.

"They found him! Robbie's home!" Hasina said.

Sydney planted her hands on her desk and rose as Charles entered.

"I hear Robbie's home. It was all over the news this morning," Charles said.

"Yeah, I know. It's great."

"Wait. Sydney. You look awful."

"I don't feel so well, but I'll be fine."

"Why don't you rest a bit. I'll call and have them reassign your room, okay?"

"Thanks, but I'll do it."

Gradually, she made her way to the nurse's station. When she approached, everyone stopped talking and turned in her direction. Looks of horror, contorted expressions, and faces riddled with repulsion quietly assaulted her. Sydney nodded, the same as she did every day.

"Come here, Dr. Chang," one of the nurses said. Sydney hobbled over. On the computer screen, Inger came into view. It was the rape scene. The blond boy's eyes were wide open in horror, tears streaming down his fire-red cheeks as Inger pushed his way into his frail body.

"Holy shit! Did anyone call the police?" Sydney gasped and looked around. Blank stares. Silent weeping. Hyperventilating breaths.

"No, not yet. We called hospital security," a nurse said.

"Call nine-one-one, now!" Sydney said and picked up the wall phone. She dialed the number that she'd memorized.

"Detective Thomas—Sydney Chang, here," she said.

"Hello, Doctor. What can I do for you?"

"You need to get to the hospital ASAP. Third floor, office building, Dr. Robert Inger's office. We're also calling nine-one-one. We have a video. He's a pedophile."

The crescendoing chatter reached a deafening peak. "Get a grip, everyone. There are patients to tend to," Sydney said.

"Dr. Chang, are you feeling okay?" a nurse asked.

"Fine. Thanks."

She was hunched over; fatigue and pain were winning. As she lumbered toward Inger's office, a rising tide of outrage permeated the corridors. Turning a corner onto his floor, she saw a crowd of nurses, PPAs, and housekeeping staff positioned in front of his door. Grace was among them. Disbelief, disgust, and outrage were drawn all over their faces. Sydney stopped. Grace nodded at her from a distance.

"Good morning, Sydney," Inger said as he passed her from behind.

Sneers and *tsk*s started quietly then built up into a rapid succession of hisses. A woman's voice called out, "You're disgusting." A dark flush of crimson stained Inger's face and neck. He moved through the crowd.

"We saw what you did," an older female voice yelled at him. Inger stopped. His eyes bulged. Bending his head, he pushed through. They crowded him. His hand shook as he placed his key into the doorknob.

"We know what you are," a male voice bellowed. Inger opened the door, squirming inside. The angry crowd continued to taunt.

Detective Thomas rounded the corner. Five police officers trailed.

Sydney peeled herself from the wall following them into the suite. She lowered herself into an empty seat at a secretary's desk. Thomas banged on Inger's office door.

"Dr. Inger. Open up. It's the NYPD," he hollered.

No response.

"We know you're in there. Open up, Doctor. Right now," he said. "Call security. Get the battering ram."

"I can help with that," said Jimmy McClary, head of security, as he moved through the crowd to the door. Jimmy had at least twenty keys on his chain. He tried one, then another.

"Don't you have the master?" Thomas asked.

"These are the master keys, but each area has its own key. Almost there. I'll get it in a minute," he replied calmly.

Two keys later, Thomas shot Sydney a look. Jimmy opened the door. Thomas and his team entered; Jimmy trailed behind.

"He's unconscious," Thomas shouted from inside Inger's office. Sydney dropped her head, placed her hands on the desk, and pushed to a stand.

"Move. Get a code cart," she whispered as loudly as she could into the crowd. With Herculean effort, she pushed past the police entering Inger's office.

Inger was on the floor with a needle in his arm. Sydney bent down and checked his pulse. None. The code cart arrived; she grabbed the Ambu bag and began breathing for him. "Nancy, do chest compressions," she said with a resigned sigh. Nancy looked at her with wide eyes, dropping her chin.

"Just do it, Nancy, now," she exhaled. Nancy dropped to her knees and started. "Narcan. Someone get it."

"Really?" a male voice asked.

"Really. Come on, people, let's just do this," Sydney replied.

Sydney started an IV line and injected the Narcan. Twelve minutes later, they called the code—Inger revived. His eyes opened—frightened, searching eyes. Sydney stared into them.

"Everyone knows," she whispered.

"Would you like me to call his family, Detective?" Jimmy asked Thomas. Inger's head swung toward Jimmy.

"We'll do it," he replied. "And, Dr. Chang, I'd like to talk to you," Thomas said.

"Not now, Detective," she said.

"Where are you going?" he asked.

"Emergency room," she said, clutching her right side.

Fifty-Seven

SOAKED IN ACRID sweat, her back was propped against the elevator wall when she slipped her hand inside her scrub top and removed the plastic cylinder from her chest. Her knees buckled. The doors parted onto the emergency room floor. Mr. Leon, an older PPA, someone whom Sydney had met when she'd first arrived, stood waiting to enter.

"Dr. Chang! Oh my goodness," he said.

"I'm okay, Mr. Leon," she croaked.

"No problem, Doc, no problem. I'm on it," he said as he took two giant steps toward her wrapping his arm around her waist. "You shakin' me up, here, Doc."

"I'm fine." Her head hung low on her chest.

His right arm placed firmly under hers and around her waist, he half carried, half dragged her out of the elevator, through the automatic doors and into the ER.

"Nurse Johnson. Look here, this is Dr. Chang," he called out to the triage nurse when they entered the nurse's station. He gently lowered Sydney into a chair at the desk.

"Cracked ribs. Maybe a pneumothorax," Sydney said to the nurse.

"We'll take care of this ASAP," the nurse said.

By the fourth morning, Sydney felt better. She eyed the hospital room with appreciation, a single with an open river view. She flipped on the television to see if the news coverage included anything about the scandal. *Nothing about Inger, only Robbie's return. How's that possible? Why are the cops holding back that information?*

Sydney reached for the heavy hospital phone by her bed and grimaced. The side-reach plus lifting the heavy phone caused a knifelike pain in her right rib area.

"Hasina, sorry I didn't call sooner. I've been sick. How's Robbie?" Sydney asked.

"I thank God he's back. He's quiet," Hasina said with a cracked voice. "Are you okay?"

"Yes. Is it possible for me to say hello to him?"

"I guess. Hang on."

"Hullllo," Robbie whispered.

"Hey, bud. How ya doing?"

"Okay."

"Glad you're home. It's over now, Robbie. You're safe."

Silence.

"Are you resting or playing with your Xbox?"

Dead air.

"Did your mom make you your favorite, grilled cheese with pickles?"

"No."

"Did she make you a milk shake?"

"Yes."

"Okay, well, I want to see you as soon as I can. Will you be ready to blade and get some Chinese food with me?"

"Uh-huh."

The sun shone as Sydney rested her head on the soft white pillow, eyes glued to the outside endless sky. She closed her eyes and within minutes fell back into a deep sleep. When she awoke, Detective Thomas was staring down at her.

"Good morning," he said.

"Detective. How long have you been standing there?"

"A few minutes. I didn't wanna wake you," he said. "I understand you had a motorcycle accident a few nights ago. Tough break. Where'd it happen?" he asked.

"Upstate New York. Take a seat," Sydney said.

"You ride there a lot?"

"In the summer. You guys did a great job finding Robbie. Thanks," she said.

"We had outside help."

"Really?"

"Yeah. Just a few miles away from where we found Robbie Wagner, we found that boy who was talking to Robbie in the hospital. He was in a house in Connecticut along with seven other kids. They said there was a person who helped them, someone they all call 'the Ninja Person.' Odd, right?"

"Ninja? Where are the kids now?"

"All the kids are in foster care. By the way, Doc, we found Robbie on Sunday night. What were you doing that night?"

"You're kidding, right?"

"Just for the record."

"Okay. There was a problem with my motorcycle in the morning; the Red Hot Ducati shop loaned me a bike, and I was riding upstate."

"You were riding after your accident. You felt well enough?"

"I felt fine until I didn't," she said.

"So if I check the E-Z Pass feeds, you'll be on them."

"I should be."

"All right, then. I'll check. When I heard of your accident, well, I was concerned."

Sydney's pager went off. It was her mother's number. *She rarely pages. Lily must be missing again.*

"Anyway, we're trying to find this 'ninja.' So if you have anything to add, you have my number. Please use it."

Thomas took three steps toward the door, then swung his head around and shot her a mischievous grin.

"Lily. What's up?"

"Mom's missing!" Lily screamed into the phone in her deep smoker's voice.

"Stop the hysteria, Lily."

"She didn't come home last night!"

"Calm down. Mom's a grown woman, and she doesn't have to answer to you. Maybe she decided to go to Atlantic City. She's done that a million times, so chill."

"And I haven't heard from David in two days."

"He must be on a binge. It's happened before. Lily, I'm in the hospital—as a patient. What do you want?"

"There's a problem. David was gonna get me a ring. He was gonna buy me a ring because we got engaged."

"So?"

"We just wanted the ring. We didn't think it was a big deal. We just needed about five thousand dollars for the ring. We waited, you know, 'til Robbie was found. We didn't want to interfere with the investigation."

"Wait. You needed five thousand dollars, and now you're telling me that Mom and David are both missing? What did you do, LILY? No! Stop talking."

Fifty-Eight

SYDNEY RIPPED OUT her IV.

"Please don't do that," said her floor nurse, Jane, as she moved toward Sydney.

"I'm keeping in the chest tube, don't worry. Please help me throw some gauze and tape on here and slip the scrub top on. I need the AMA release form too, please," Sydney said.

When the nurse exited, Sydney paged Smikes, asking for a wheelchair and a ride.

"You sure you okay to leave? You don't look so good," he said five minutes later as he rolled her out.

"Very sure."

"Well...okay." Smikes hesitated, then strolled toward the building, glancing back twice. Sydney waited. When she was sure that he was gone, she stepped out of the chair, pushed it aside, and walked around the block to the motorcycle that she had parked a few days earlier. She pulled two parking tickets out of the crack where the tank and seat met then pushed them into her pants pocket.

LILY CRACKED OPEN the door with coiffed hair and magenta-colored eye shadow, blush, and lipstick. The contrast against her sallow complexion made her look egg-yolk yellow. Her frail body was engulfed in the usual hot pink–and-orange flannel pajamas with matching-colored knitted wool slippers. *Ninety-eight degrees outside, and she's in flannel and wool.*

"We didn't think it would be a big deal, Syd, we didn't," Lily blurted as Sydney marched in past her. "But now Mom and David are missing."

"What's not a big deal? What did you do, Lily?" Sydney asked through gritted teeth. *She's mentally ill. BREATHE.*

"David asked the guy we followed for money." Lily hung her head.

"What guy?"

"The guy we followed to Gramercy Park, the one from the town house in the West Village. We figured he'd have money—you know, Gramercy Park is pretty wealthy, so, well…," she said and continued to stare at her feet.

"You WHAT?" *Mom warned me: "Whatever you do, don't involve Lily or David."*

"But we waited until Robbie was safe. We just needed some money for the engagement ring, and we didn't think—"

"That's right. You didn't think. You only think about yourself, Lily."

"David asked me to marry him. And I'm trying to help now! I'm thinking about Mom and David now. Nothing ever works out for me. I'm so tired of this shit."

"You're crying about a ring and marriage? What about David? You selfish piece of…arghhh." *Did David give me up? Even if he did, what's it got to do with my mom? If they were taken, did this Gramercy guy do it himself, or did he call the trafficking ring? The ring is bigger—the guy who messed up my bike is still out there—but how much bigger?*

"But, but things were going so great with David and me, and now this."

"Maybe you should have thought about the consequences *before* you tried to blackmail a rich pedophile."

Fifty-Nine

SYDNEY WAS BENT over in front of the Gramercy address that Lily had provided, her hands rummaging through the garbage cans. With a cap pulled down low on her forehead, bright red lipstick and large sunglasses, she waded through a sea of wet and smelly junk. Digging deeper, she found an envelope and then felt something solid; she extricated two magazines—*The Economist* and *Business Insider*. Cleaning them off with her gloved hands, she read the addressee's name: Steven Behrens.

In Union Square Park, her search showed that he was the CFO of Martin Lane Securities. The public record revealed that Mr. Behrens had earned eighteen million, twenty million, and twenty-four million dollars in compensation over the past three years. *Is he just a pedophilic john who called someone to handle David, or is he part of the ring? With that kind of money, I doubt he's anything more than a john.*

"THE DOORMAN JUST brought up a brown box. Should I open it?" Lily asked as Sydney grabbed her home phone.

"Do you hear any ticking?"

"Wait. I'll check." Pause. "No, I don't think so."

"Don't open it. Keep it in the hallway. I'm coming now."

Lily was pacing when Sydney exited the elevator. The box sat a few feet away by the stairwell.

"Whaddaya think's in there?" Lily said.

Sydney bent placing her ear to the cardboard, listening for ticking or weird noises. Gloved, on her knees now, wet wipe in hand, she removed Lily's prints from the box and sliced open the shiny packing tape. Inside were a manila envelope and a throwaway cell phone. She walked it into the apartment. Lily followed. The beige envelope held two white letter-sized envelopes. Sydney slid the knife into the first, pulling out a photo. It was David. She closed her eyes, bowed her head, and took a deep breath. He was splayed out on a grungy brown bedspread in what looked like a seedy motel, a needle hanging from his arm. His head was tipped back, his mouth open, with spittle down the left side of his blue-tinged face. He looked dead. *Shit.* The second envelope held a thick three-inch square slice of human skin with an angel tattoo on it.

Sydney glanced at her sister. Lily drank milky iced coffee at the card-sized kitchen table while thumbing through a fashion magazine. The Home Shopping Network showcased a pair of red strappy stilettos on the mini-television in front of her. *Typical Lily. Always looking for new clothes—no matter what.*

"What kind of tattoo does David have on his arm, Lily?"

"Uh, an angel, I think. Yeah, an angel." Lily took a sip from her stripped straw. *Crap. Definitely dead.*

"Why?" she asked, turning another page.

"I'm going to find Mom. If we aren't home by noon tomorrow, call Cousin Andy and ask him to come get you. Stay in Toronto with him. Don't call your funereal school until you're in Canada. And, Lily, whatever you do, don't tell Andy what happened over the phone. Wait until you see him in person. Understand?"

"I don't wanna go to Canada," she said; her head started bobbing. Her eyes were opening and closing.

"If we're not back, you'll have no choice."

"But I don't wanna go," Lily said and nodded off, her head casting to the left.

The phone inside the box rang. Sydney waited. On the fifth ring she answered. "Yes," she said, half covering the mouthpiece.

"Is this Dr. Sydney Chang?" a male voice asked through a synthesizer.

"Who wants to know?"

"Dr. Chang?"

"What do you want?"

"We have her. And if you don't want her to end up like the man, I suggest you do what I say."

Sydney waited.

"We want all the original DVDs and flash drives and the money, all three hundred thousand, in one hour."

"Not possible. I'll need five."

"I'll be generous and give you two. I'll call at eight thirty."

"I want to speak to her."

Click. Sydney ripped the battery out of the phone. *Not the Behrens guy. He'd want the information but wouldn't know or care about the money. He's too rich. When David threatened him, he must have called someone connected to Inger or Fenly or the Connecticut people, someone who would know about the empty vault and the originals. Why is he specifically asking for the originals, though? Fingerprints?*

In her mother's bedroom, Sydney found the box of money exactly where she'd expected her mother to hide it, on the top shelf of the bedroom closet under the blankets. She stuffed the untouched bills into a duffel bag. Despite Sydney's insistence that they were both illegal and dangerous, her mother's stash of firecrackers sat nestled in their usual place. *They killed David. They'll kill Mom, too.*

In the hallway right outside of her mother's apartment, Sydney located the vent that she'd visited a few days before when she dropped the money off. She set a stool underneath it and stretched her arm into the black passageway. She pulled out another duffel bag, opened it, and checked the contents: wig, makeup, bulletproof vest, throwing star, expandable baton, stiletto knife, two remote-operated detonators, dart gun, and untraceable revolver.

Calling the cops or asking Johnny is out. They choose the location. They'll have a spotter. If I'm not alone, they'll kill her immediately and leave. They'll want info from me about anyone else involved before they kill us. They'll use her as leverage. Either I finish them first, or we lose. I'll need a distraction to improve my chances.

Making a quick run into the kitchen, she grabbed a bottle of bleach and a glass quart bottle, dumped the fizzy water, and headed back to her mother's room. Unwrapping the firecrackers, she duct-taped them around the base of the glass bottle and left with Lily passed out, her head resting on the magazine.

Sixty

SYDNEY TOSSED THE $100,000 into the kitchen washing machine in her apartment. She poured in detergent and pressed start. She turned on her laser color printer. She grabbed a block of white typing paper, a paper cutter, a metal ruler, and an X-ACTO knife. She taped five $100 bills to the paper. The printer produced approximately thirty-five ppm, and in the time she had, she figured she could easily turn out about four hundred copies of five $100 bills—$200,000 in fakes.

Ninety minutes later, she inserted $50,000 of the freshly laundered and dried money, the Inger flash drive, and a note into a plain paper bag. It read:

> Here's $50,000, and a preview of what's on your DVDs. If you want the rest of the money and the original drives, we'll have to meet. Bring her intact.

She wove the other half of the real bills into the fake ones and stuffed six four-inch mixed stacks and the DVDs and flash drives into a metal briefcase.

It was 7:55 P.M., thirty-five minutes until the next call. She injected a local anesthetic around her chest tube site for at least three hours of relief. Sydney applied a light-colored foundation on her face, neck, and ears. She slipped clothing on over her bulletproof vest. A baseball cap, leather gloves, and steel-toed work boots completed her biker look. Her accessories and helmet were in one backpack. The money and data were in another. She carried an extra helmet for her mom.

Sydney surveyed the streets, riding up and down the teen-numbered ones and then into the east twenties. Near a housing project, she spotted it: an old Honda motorcycle, one of the neighborhood bikes. It was parked on a poorly lit, desolate street under a sturdy tree at the end of a block, one block west of the East River. She checked for street cameras. She pulled her bike into a spot four blocks away and siphoned some gas from its tank into the firecracker-rigged glass bottle. *Not the best use of my chemistry major.* After recapping it, she walked back to the Honda and sat on the curb. Sydney slipped the battery back into the phone and waited. Eight twenty-two P.M.

At eight thirty, the phone pinged.

"Everything in order?" he asked.

"Yes," she said.

"Meet me at—"

"No meet-up until I speak to her. Put her on."

Fumbling and static assaulted Sydney's ear, then silence and heavy breathing.

"Sydney?" her mother asked in a hoarse voice.

"You okay?"

"Don't worry. You know I'll be fine. Do what you need to do."

Her eyes narrowed. Her pulse pounded. Hot fury coursed down her body and charged back up into her chest and throat.

"You have one hour to drop off the package with my stuff at two-thirty Fulton Avenue in Yonkers."

She scribbled.

"Take the NY Thruway North to Exit 5. Take NY-100 North/Central Park Ave toward White Plains. Exit at Midland Avenue. Turn right onto Midland, then right onto Fulton. On the right, there's a storage facility. There'll be a garbage can next to a mailbox in the middle of six long buildings. Leave the package between the garbage can and the mailbox. Nine thirty sharp."

Sixty-One

SYDNEY LOOKED FOR pedestrians—none. She smacked some appliqués onto her helmet then altered the old Honda's license plate. Two gloved fingers followed the wires from the keyed ignition down to a plug-in, near the engine. She unsnapped it and mounted the bike. From her pants pocket, she removed a piece of wire; the ends were stripped, exposing metal. She maneuvered it into the bike's uncovered ignition slots until she heard a click. She pushed the start button, and the engine roared to life.

Sydney drove up the FDR Drive. Traffic was light. In Yonkers, she made three quick turns and approached a row of weathered white storage buildings. Crooked red-and-yellow signs dangled from the middle of each unit.

Yonkers Self Storage
The Affordable, Smart Storage Solution

The sign on the post read: 230 FULTON AVE. There were no street lamps, just six spotlights each directed at a building entrance. The surrounding expanse of leafy trees cast billowy shadows of surreal images onto the smooth metal buildings; it looked like an abandoned set from a Hitchcock movie.

Sydney steered the bike in and around each building until she spotted the mailbox and garbage can between buildings two and three. She dismounted, looked left and right—not a person in sight. A few bashed soda cans rolled across the pavement in the wind. *Crash!* She swiveled. A wire mesh garbage can several yards away was on its side. Three mangy stray cats were on the run. She pivoted. Dirty, yellowed newspapers flew about as she moved toward the drop point. There between the garbage can and mailbox sat a black dog, a Labrador retriever. She froze. He stood. She was about five feet away. He took a step toward her. She remained still. He took another step, and she saw it—a cardboard sign around his neck. There was writing on it. Black lettering highlighted by green glow-in-the-dark ink: TRANSFER THE ITEMS INTO MY BACKPACK AND LEAVE.

The dog sniffed her leg. She opened the paper bag. Slowly, she placed individual cash stacks into his pack then zipped it. The dog's front paws stiffened. He froze, turned his head, looked behind him, and within seconds tore off into the woods behind the storage facility.

With the disposable phone in her hip pocket, she drove three blocks, pulled off the road, and waited in a dark patch on a side street. 9:33.

10:08. The phone vibrated.

"Where's the rest of the money and the original drives?" he asked.

"The rest will come when I get what I want."

"Meet me at one-forty Clearland Street in ten minutes."

"And she'll be there?"

"The rest of the money and the original drives."

"Bring her intact."

"Bring me what you owe me."

Click.

She examined her street map. The address was two blocks away. She pushed her bike into the woods, where it was well hidden, and opened her backpack.

SET BACK IN the dark deserted parking lot was a crumbling warehouse. A tattered sign on the building read:

> PR Industries
> The answer to all your paper good needs.

Wearing a full-faced helmet, she advanced. The evening air smelled like wood pulp, sour. Her eyes scanned the rooftops, estimating the dimensions of the building. It was about one hundred feet wide; depth unclear, maybe thirty feet tall, with white opaque wire-reinforced windows rimming the building approximately twenty-five feet off the ground. Three of those push-out windows were slightly open. Four small lights bolted to the roof's rim lit the front of the building. The building was perfect for spotters.

The main door was on the left side. She fake-stumbled near the building's wall, opening her left hand. The Molotov cocktail slid down her arm out of her sleeve onto the ground against the side of the building. She placed it out of the sight line of three humming surveillance cameras moving back and forth; one above the door, the other two on each corner of the building. Sydney rose, standing in front of the steel door. She located a round white buzzer affixed to the side with masking tape and pressed it twice. *Click.* The door unlocked.

Inhaling, she pushed the door open into a dim, dank anteroom illuminated by shreds of light flowing in from the high windows. *No hesitation.* Her helmet's tinted face mask made it difficult to see. Lifting the hinge emitted a slight squeak that echoed through the quiet building. Sydney entered slowly, one foot forward, then the next. The room was empty. Her eyes darted in search of her mother. She spotted a doorway to the right. Moving toward it, a cavernous space, about fifty feet deep and eighty feet wide, came into view. A catwalk encircled the inner perimeter about twenty feet above. Only two rays of light pierced the darkness: one from a single low-wattage bulb that hung from the ceiling at the far left of the room, the other from a spotlight. The round spot, about twelve inches in diameter, shone onto an immobile object that sat three quarters of the way back, about thirty feet from the doorway. She stepped toward it. Two steps closer and she knew. Her mother sat bound to a small fold-up chair; glints of light bounced off of the whites of her blinking eyes. She was alive.

"Stop. Drop the briefcase," a male voice instructed from behind on her far right. She turned, but it was too dark to make out his features.

Sydney placed the case on the floor in front of her. A red laser dot appeared on the left side of her mom's chest. *Someone's up top, too. Shit.* Ripping off her helmet, her head was bowed; her eyes lifted to find her mother's. They made eye contact; Sydney lowered her lids and tipped her head.

"Where's my stuff?" the man asked, moving closer, out of the shadows. Sydney glanced out of the corner of her eye. He held a pistol in his right hand, finger on the trigger, aiming at her head.

"Here," Sydney said, squatting, clicking the case open, and surreptitiously unsnapping the bottom compartment. "I have copies. When you release my mother, I'll take you to them."

"Who helped you in Connecticut?"

"Let my mother go, and I'll tell you."

"How's your bike? Having any trouble with it?"

"So you're the ass who messed with it," she said.

"Tell me who helped you or your mother will suffer."

Sydney grabbed the pistol taped between her shoulder blades, simultaneously hitting the button in her pants pocket. *BOOM!* The explosion blew open the front door as Sydney fired a shot into her mother's chest. Her mother fell back. *Leverage gone.* A shot whizzed by Sydney's face.

Sydney reached into the case, opening the false bottom, and pulled out a 9mm Beretta. She rolled and shot. Blood spewed from the man's abdomen as he collapsed to the floor.

In her jacket, Sydney pressed another button, and a loud hiss emanated from the case. Three seconds later, firecracker shells shot into the air, exploding into red and green starbursts above the catwalk. The warehouse turned into a Christmas-meets–July Fourth kaleidoscopic display. Simultaneously, Sydney fired three shots up toward the catwalk in the direction of the laser stream. Bullets slammed into the cement floor as she raced toward her mother. As the embers dropped from the sky, smoke filled the air.

Rapid footfalls clattered down a metal staircase in the back of the room. She shot toward the sound. Driving her mother's chair back out of the spotlight to the right corner of the room, a bullet slammed into Sydney's back.

"Ohhhh," she exhaled. She lurched forward. She landed on her mother's chair. She was still. Then she shook her head. *Get up! NOW!* Positioned between the bullets and her mother, she fired over her shoulder: two shots, then a click. Her gun was empty. *He must have heard that.* She pushed a button, and her clip dropped. The footsteps closed in. Panting and heavy breathing approached. Turning, she threw a *shuriken*.

"Shit," he said.

Bang! The impact of the bullet into her left side knocked the breath out of her as she staggered and dropped to one knee. *His next shot will be a head shot.* She lunged up and barreled into him. His weapon clanked to the floor as he fought to remain standing. In that split second, she saw his face. Jimmy McClary, the head security guard at the hospital. She hesitated.

He tackled her, landing on top. He held her in a three-point pin, his legs pinning her arms down and his hands tightening around her neck. He squeezed. She threw a leg crossover, but he was big. He squeezed harder. Her eyelids fluttered. Her air supply diminished. Grabbing his thumb, she tried to break it, but he ground his knee into her bicep. Sydney popped her hips up, lifting her legs, and clamped them around his neck in a death grip. Her rock-hard calves pressed together. His grip loosened. The air moved. She took a raspy breath.

A shot rang out, then another; the man with the abdominal wound was up and moving toward her. She grabbed Jimmy as a shield, and the impact of the bullet smashing into his torso forced her back. She ripped the *shuriken* out of Jimmy's shoulder and winged it toward the shooter. Another bullet slammed into the wall behind them as Sydney rolled and came up shooting Jimmy's gun. Aiming toward the shooter, she emptied the clip. Two bullets slammed into his chest. *Done.*

Jimmy's breathing was ragged. His eyes were wide open. She bent over him.

"Help me. Please, Sydney," he whispered. She stared. Blood spurted rhythmically into the air. Each spray lessened until it stopped about a minute later.

Sydney ran over to her mother, checked her pulse, and cut her loose. Her mother's eyes fluttered open. Sydney gently removed the tranquilizer dart from her mother's right chest.

Sixty-Two

"I JUST WANTED the ring, that's all. I didn't think it was going to cause all of this commotion," Lily said as she poured herself a cup of coffee and took a seat at the kitchen table.

"I'm putting together a bigger team of professionals for you, Lily. I'll get you better help. You need it. But that's it. Hear me loud and clear. I'm not coming out to rescue you anymore," Sydney said.

Lily poured more sugar into her coffee.

"How's your chest, Mom?" Sydney asked.

"Sore. You shot me."

"Sorry, but I didn't want them to torture you."

"You and your sister have been torturing me for years. What difference does it make?" her mom said.

BREAKING NEWS: Pedophilic ring video footage surfaces

flashed on the tiny television screen. Sydney turned up the volume.

"New video footage shows several high-profile individuals in compromising positions tied to the pedophilic ring associated with the hospital kidnapping of the rescued seven-year-old boy. The tape includes Dr. Robert Inger, the physician from Manhattan Hospital charged with pedophilia and murder last week, and Steven Behrens, a New York City venture capitalist, found dead in the trunk of a parked car in back of a Yonkers warehouse. Two other men found dead in this Yonkers warehouse last night are also tied to this case: Jimmy McClary, the head of security at Manhattan Hospital and Peter Regent, the owner of the warehouse. Both were high school classmates of Dr. Inger's. As more of the story unfolds, we will bring it to you."

Sixty-Three

THE ENVELOPE DIDN'T have a return address. Sydney held it up to the light. She thought about it for a few seconds then opened it with care. It held a check wrapped in a white piece of paper, no note. Mick sat beside her, his long legs stretched out on the couch in his photography studio.

"Wow. My friend Johnny just sent us a check for three hundred fifty thousand dollars," Sydney said. *He gave us $50,000 more than we found at the Connecticut house.*

"Here, Atsuko. Please add this in," Sydney said and handed it to her. Atsuko's friends were generous as well. She'd had over thirty contributions as of yesterday.

Mick turned to face Sydney, his deep hazel eyes full of wonder. "That's some friend. Is Johnny a doctor too?" he asked.

"No. Just an old friend."

"Some friend," he said again.

"Very exciting, very nice," Atsuko said.

"Atsuko, did you get the check from Grace and her church that I left for you at the front desk?" Sydney asked.

"Yes, yes. So nice."

The buzzer rang. Sydney ushered in a few children accompanied by adults. It was eleven months since she'd rescued the eight children from the house in Connecticut. Six were present today with social workers and foster care guardians. The two youngest were the only ones lucky enough to reunite with their parents, located thanks to a huge effort from Detective Thomas and Mick.

The kids had met with Sydney and Mick only once before. At that time, Sydney explained that after reading about them in the paper, she came up with an idea that she wanted to discuss with them. She spoke about working together to find "forever homes" for each of them. Homes with nice parents; parents that wouldn't make them do things that hurt their bodies. When she asked if they wanted to participate, each child slowly nodded in agreement. "When do we start?" asked the blond boy, Daniel.

The children stood in silence, their enlarged eyes darting around the room, soaking in the plethora of cameras, lights, and backdrops. Mick picked up a camera and in an animated way explained the viewfinder, then moved on to the lens and shutter release. When he finished his quick lesson, Sydney noticed an engaged, happy glint in some of their eyes.

Atsuko, Grace, and Detective Thomas stood in the back of the room as Mick began the photo shoot, posing the children together and separately. He cracked goofy jokes, and after a few minutes the six-foot-three-inch photojournalist turned cautious giggles into bouts of laughter. Sydney's hand tapped her thigh to the blasting Beyoncé music. Atsuko tapped her high-heeled shiny red shoe. Detective Thomas's eyes were filled, and he blinked every few seconds.

When the last frame was shot and the bright lights were switched off, Sydney stood in front of the kids holding a black sign with white lettering.

BREATHE, FOCUS, DO FOUNDATION

She addressed the children: "Ladies and gentlemen, I am proud to announce that our foundation, the one I told you about a few months ago, officially opened today. Many thanks to Mick, Atsuko, Detective Thomas, Grace, all of you great kids, and wonderful social workers and foster guardians. We're on a mission! And when we breathe, focus, and do, we can accomplish anything, right, kids?"

"Right!" they called out.

"We can't wait to find your 'forever homes,'" Sydney said. "And with these fantastic photos, we've started the ball rolling!"

The foundation also provided complete financial assistance for mental and physical health care; their educational expenses were covered until the age of twenty-three. Sydney wanted to provide loving people with the heart, but not necessarily the funds, an unencumbered and speedy route to adopting a child with needs.

"I'll have these great photos posted on our website by tonight so the whole world can see how cool you guys are," Mick said.

"What's the latest number of pro bono child psychiatrists participating?" Detective Thomas whispered into Sydney's ear.

"Sixteen and growing."

"Excellent. You're something," he said and grinned at her.

Atsuko approached the children with bright green gift bags. "Just a little something from Japan. Fun, very fun." The kid's faces lit up as they reached in to find handheld electronic games. Atsuko walked over to Sydney. "This one is for Robbie-san. Please give him."

"Will do. Thank you, Atsuko," Sydney said.

After pizza and soda, the children and their companions left.

Atsuko turned to Thomas. "Detective, I have party at my house on Saturday night. Can you make it?" she asked.

"I'd love to."

"Sydney, I know you don't go to parties, but will you make exception? Grace and her husband are coming," Atsuko said.

Sydney grinned. "We'll be there, Atsuko."

"We will?" Mick asked, tilting his head as he ran his hand through his thick black hair. Detective Thomas's head spun. He stared at Sydney.

"What makes you think you're part of that 'we,' buddy?" Sydney said as she slipped her hand into his.

Sixty-four

SKATING UP THE Avenue of the Americas, Sydney enjoyed the pleasant July breeze on her face. A skinny man with scraggly hair, tattered jeans, and a ripped T-shirt ran across Eighth Street right in front of her. In the crook of his arm, he clutched an expensive-looking tote bag, something like Lily and Atsuko carried. She braked. Two police officers followed, chasing. Sydney stopped and watched. The gap grew wider. Wider. Sydney swerved right onto Eighth Street and sped up to the officers.

"Want help?" she asked.

THE END

Acknowledgements

WITH SPECIAL THANKS to my pillars: Jimmy, Harriet, HSY, Lisa J, James, Devan, Ben, Hamilton, Rebecca, and Fran W.

Author's Note

HUMAN TRAFFICKING may be occurring right down the street from you. If you suspect that it is, here is some information to help you get help. Thank you for caring.

National Human Trafficking Hotline—1-888-373-7888 or go to:

> https://humantraffickinghotline.org/report-trafficking
> http://sharedhope.org/join-the-cause/report-trafficking/
> https://2001-2009.state.gov/g/tip/rls/fs/34563.htm
> https://polarisproject.org/recognize-signs

BUT if you or someone you know is in immediate danger, call 911.

If you enjoyed *Sydney On Fire*, please spread the word by writing a review on Amazon.com.

Sydney lives on at www.sydneyonfire.com.

Thanks!! B. B.

About the Author

B. B. CARY lives under the radar in New York City.

Made in United States
North Haven, CT
24 January 2024